Royalty and Ruin

Modern Magick, 5

Charlotte E. English

1

Right, crash course on troll culture.

Ye Olde Historic Record shows that they originated up Scandinavia way (at least, so it's claimed. This is academia. Naturally there are those who strenuously disagree). If that's the case, they wasted no time in spreading across the rest of Europe, and rather beyond. The oldest known troll enclaves in Britain date back to before the Roman conquest.

The brutal truth is, they are a bit cleverer than we are. A truly embarrassing number of magickal developments have been fairly laid to the trolls' credit (for example, anyone who tells you that humans developed the flying chair trick is either misinformed or a liar — and my pretty Sunstone Wand was most certainly a troll masterpiece).

Still, at least we have the Book. Dear Mauf, or Bill as he was previously known; that marvellous construct that absorbs knowledge like a sponge, and then spits it out again in exquisitely refined nineteenth-century English. The creator of said book might have been a shady character, but at least she was human.

Then again, the Troll Court-that-was, Farringale, managed to purloin that one, and already I hear people adding Mauf's invention to the trolls' record of marvels. Maybe this is really how it works. It isn't that they are so much brighter than we are. It's that they have really, really good PR.

Anyway. Trolls are clever, and steeped in magick up to their enormous eyeballs. They're physically superior, more sophisticated than most people think (and by an order of magnitude), and — a point which will ever endear them to my heart — they are spectacularly good at food. Mandridore, the Royal Court of the Trolls since the mid seventeenth century, is the most powerful of the Fae Courts by a wide margin, too.

And they know it. Some would accuse our troll compatriots of possessing just a smidgeon in the way of arrogance. And they would not be wrong. But, well, with so many advantages as they enjoy it's hard to blame them for being self-satisfied. I mean, wouldn't you be?

I may be a cosmopolitan woman of the world, with over a decade of high adventure behind me, but I admit to experiencing some small sensations of trepidation upon departing for my introduction at this particular Court. Meeting royalty hasn't been part of my general duties to date, and *these* royals…! I'm a mere human. I am not up to this.

'Yes, you are,' said Jay, informing me of two things at once: one, that he's a good sort, ready with the kind of staunch back-up one needs at a time like this. Two, that I had been talking to myself like a ninny.

Good start.

'Of course I am,' I said stoutly, and stood a bit taller. 'And so are you.'

'Naturally.' It was fifty-six minutes past four in the afternoon and we were waiting for the Baron to arrive. Jay had taken up a lounging posture in an oversized armchair which had, apparently, appeared in the great hall at Home just for that purpose. I didn't recall seeing it before. Jay flashed me the firm, confident smile of a man who knows no fear.

'You're petrified, aren't you?' I said.

'I had to sit down. Somebody's replaced my kneecaps with jelly.'

I subjected him to a swift, professional survey. I've learned that Jay tends to overcompensate; the more nervous he is, the more confident he appears. But if you didn't know that about him, nothing about his languid posture would tip you off.

He was wearing a suit. *Jay in a suit!* Wise man, he had gone for a muted blue colour, with a waistcoat and everything. It set off his dark skin handsomely, and he'd done something intriguing to his black hair.

'You look dishy,' I told him.

'Dishy.'

'Yes.'

'No one has used that word since about 1953.'

'And you are insufficiently quiffed to merit the term? I see your point.' Actually, the Danny Zuko quiff-and-jacket combo would suit Jay down to the ground, but I kept that thought to myself.

He grinned at me, and eyed my dress, then my hair. The former was a violet silk confection with a subdued (for me, anyway) knot work print in bejewelled colours. The latter was golden — not golden-blonde but actually pale gold — and loosely piled up on my head. Well, if there is a day for looking respectably drab and anaemic it certainly isn't the day you're whisked off to the heights of royal luxury.

'You look bonny,' said Jay.

'Which no one has said since 1927.'

'I am absolutely certain they did not have dresses like that in 1927.'

'Says who? They were wild back then. Short hems and everything.' Not that my dress was short. It was swishily long — I prefer that term to the soulless "maxi dress" — but it did leave me just a bit bare about the shoulder area.

Gravel crunched on the driveway outside as a sizeable car purred to a stop by the doors. A flash of glossy mulberry-coloured paintwork caught my eye.

'Here we go,' I said, collecting my shoulder-bag.

'You aren't taking that?' Jay did not move.

I hefted the bag. 'This? Why wouldn't I?'

Jay just looked at me.

All right, perhaps it is inconsistent to deck myself in colour and silk like a gilded butterfly and then sling my faithful old satchel over my shoulder.

'I need it.'

'You need what's in it. Surely we can find a better solution.'

I laid the bag back on the floor and looked at it. It is a purple cloth thing, a bit scuffed around the edges, and sturdy. It has a single dragonfly embroidered upon the flap. I put it there myself. Just at present, it was bulging with soft things for the pup to sleep in, underneath which lay Mauf-the-smart-mouthed-book, my Sunstone Wand (apparently I'm really not taking that back to Stores), and a variety of other necessities.

'I could make a smart suitcase of it if I had a bit more time,' I said doubtfully. I'd need to dig out the Wand, and then I'd need about half an hour. The process is a bit delicate. 'And then the flying charm — the one we use on the chairs — should take—'

I stopped talking, because with a wiggle and a shimmy my bag was changing. It flexed its seams, and with an audible *pop* it became a neat oblong case, stacked high, and tinted a soft heathery-purple. The dragonfly embroidered had become an embossed design spanning the top from edge to edge.

I rapped on the top and the lid bounced open. My tiny sunny-yellow pup smiled at me from inside, and rolled onto her back. The underside of the lid revealed a scattering of tiny air holes, invisible from the surface. 'Pup travels in style,' I said, patting her soft head before gently closing the case again.

'Nice work,' said Jay, as he sprang out of his chair (which promptly melted back into the wall).

'But, not mine.' If Jay hadn't done it, then who...? We were alone in the hall. 'Did you do that, House?'

There was no answer, precisely, but as I watched, my new case rose three feet in the air and began to glide slowly towards the door.

'You've got style, House,' I said, following my jazzy new luggage. 'Thank you.'

A sprig of gilding blossomed around the case's edges.

Baron Alban stood leaning on the bonnet of his car, arms folded, his bronzed hair gleaming in the late afternoon sun. I was encouraged to see him wearing a suit not a million miles in style from Jay's; apparently we were on the right track, at least sartorially.

His brows went up as my suitcase sailed gracefully over to the car and ensconced itself in the back seat.

'Wasn't your car green before?' I said.

The Baron smiled. 'Wasn't your hair blue before?'

'Fair point.'

'How far are we going?' said Jay as he joined my case in the back seat, having stashed his own, less airborne luggage in the boot.

'Far,' said Alban, opening the front passenger door for me. 'And not far.'

'Helpful.'

'I do try.' Having settled me in the lap of automobile luxury, Alban returned to the driver's seat and off we went. His lovely car pulled smoothly away from Home, and I permitted myself one long, wistful look back at the familiar contours of the sprawling, craggy old building before it disappeared from view. Bathed in golden sunglow as it was, it appeared to me as a vision of paradise.

We'll be back, I told myself.

Even Milady had implied as much, though she was responsible for our general expulsion from the property. 'I am in no official position to grant you leave to attend Mandridore,' she had said earlier that day. 'But I grant it anyway, upon a strictly limited basis.' In other words, come back soon.

Val had been more demonstrative. Never one for overt affection, she had fixed me with a gimlet stare and said frostily: 'So you're abandoning us for royalty.'

'Only for a bit,' I had protested.

'A bit? How long is a "bit"?'

'A while?'

Val's eyes had narrowed dangerously.

I'd broken the unspoken rules so far as to lean down and kiss her cheek. 'I'll miss you too.'

'Hmph.' Val had gone back to her laptop, ignoring me utterly.

I'd felt loved.

There had been a text from Val a bit later. *Tell the Baron. Either he brings you back in one piece, and soon, or I break his kneecaps.*

I didn't really doubt that she meant it literally.

So, the Troll Roads. These were but a recent discovery of mine. They are another of those brilliant magickal inventions the trolls are responsible for, a mingling of Waymastery magicks and goodness-knows what else. On the face of it they are not that exciting: you drive along much as normal, pootling happily down wide, well-kept roads lined with tall, flowering hedges, the boughs of an occasional overhanging oak enlivening the view. But something whooshes you along much faster than it seems, and a journey that ought to take two hours might take less than one. This was what the Baron meant by "far, but not far."

The likes of Jay and I are not normally permitted to use them; they are strictly troll-only. But in the Baron's company, all options are open. We cruised down these beautiful highways at a leisurely pace, and within an hour we turned off onto the M25. It should've taken hours to make it so far south.

'This is the London area,' I observed, at my most scintillatingly intelligent.

'So it is.' The Baron was noncommittal.

'So Mandridore's down London way?'

'One could assume that.'

'One could indeed. In fact, one has.'

No answer.

'So am I right?' I pressed.

'Wait till we stop and I'll get you an annotated map of modern Mandridore, together with a route plan down from Yorkshire.'

'Really?'

His grin flashed. 'No.'

Jay spoke up from the back seat. 'I'll remember the way.'

'Like hell you will,' said Alban.

'Watch me.'

'I'd have to kill you.'

A pause. 'All right, don't watch me.'

Mercifully, we were not condemned to linger long upon the M25. People have been known to lose patience, hope, sanity and their immortal souls by such foolishness (or ill luck) as that. The thing is, I couldn't quite say when we left the motorway, or how it happened. One minute we were flying over tarmac at ninety miles an hour; the next we were swanning along a wide, white-paved road at a much more leisurely pace, low walls of pale stone flying by us on either side, with the scents of honeysuckle and lemon hanging heavy upon the air.

'Curse you,' muttered Jay.

Baron Alban chuckled. 'I'll tell you one thing for free. Those who have pleased Their Majesties have been known to walk away with a special boon by way of a thank you. Usually you're allowed to choose.'

'Right,' said Jay. 'Challenge accepted.'

2

I WAS IN NO way surprised to find the Royal Court of Mandridore tucked away so close to London. Back in the bad old days of a few hundred years ago, London was rapidly becoming the centre of England and beyond, even if geographically speaking it was nothing of the kind. (And really, what's changed?). If you had to found a new centre of government in a hurry, where else would you put it? And it wasn't so far from the site of old Farringale, either — no more than sixty or seventy miles.

The more interesting question was: how did it fit? For London has sprawled out a long, long way over the centuries, swallowing everything in its path. But the magickal Enclaves and Dells are funny like that. It's like they occupy their own little bubbles of space, which aren't quite on the same plane of reality as the rest of Britain. There's a way in, or two, and once over the magickal threshold it's like you are in a different world.

Maybe you literally are. We've been making some odd, and enlightening, discoveries in that sort of direction lately.

Anyway. Being a magickal Dell (I guessed) as well as a Troll Enclave, Mandridore had all the usual hallmarks. There was that tantalising scent in the air, of the before-mentioned fruit and flowers, together with some indefinable but glorious aromas that made my head spin, they were so intoxicating. The air shimmered with the soft, silvery glow of twilight on the approach, though Britain proper was still bathed in bright sunshine. Tall, shapely shrubs occupied nooks just off the road; they looked like topiaries, posed in the shapes of animals or well-dressed ladies and gentlemen, but I think they were more than that. I could swear I saw one wave at us as we passed. We drove under perfumed arbours twinkling with starry lights, wove through a maze of rose-scattered hedgerows, and by the time we drew to a stop the sky had settled into a most intriguing configuration: one half was sunlit day, and the other lay dreaming under a silver moon.

'I may never leave,' I said as the Baron drew the car to a stop. We had passed several sets of ornate, silver-or-gold gates rising majestically into the skies; the Baron had paused at the sixth or seventh of these, waited as they slowly opened for us, and turned in to a sweeping, paved driveway before a handsome Elizabethan mansion. The place was built from brick, as was common for fine houses of that period; but these bricks were faintly bluish, which wasn't at all. The house had two spacious wings poised either side of a central hall, with big diamond-paned windows and those fabulous twizzly chimney pots. And it was, of course, enormous — not just in the sense of the ground it covered, but in the height and breadth of the doors, too. This mansion had been built by trolls, for trolls.

'Is this the Court?' said Jay as he got out, and stood staring doubtfully at the house.

I saw his point. Handsome as it was, it was by no means a palace, and had none of the imposing grandeur one would typically expect of a royal residence.

'No,' said Alban. 'This is Their Majesties' private home.'

'What?'

'They asked that you be brought here first, for a private audience. You will see the Court later.'

'So it's a secret assignment.' Jay did not sound pleased.

But I was. 'The best kind,' I told him.

He frowned at me.

'Oh, come on. All the most exciting things happen when you're doing things you aren't supposed to.'

The Baron spoke firmly. 'Their Majesties would never ask you to do anything lawless.'

I patted his arm. 'You said that with such total confidence. It's beautiful.'

He grimaced. 'The life of a diplomat.'

'Hobnobbing with beautiful people, swanning around in gorgeous cars, prancing from mansion to mansion, and strutting your stuff in expensive clothes? Really, a spot of lying-through-your-teeth here and there isn't so much to ask.'

He gave me the side-eye. 'Prancing?'

'Prancing.'

He squared his shoulders, making his admittedly splendid muscles ripple. 'I wouldn't dream of prancing.'

And he didn't. What he achieved on his way from car to front door was more of a manly mince.

Jay rolled his eyes, and retrieved his luggage from the boot. Mine, of course, sailed airily over to the door by itself. 'It's already a madhouse and we've been here five minutes.'

'Chin high,' I said, lifting my own by a couple of inches. 'We're important people now.'

Jay put his nose in the air, and in we went.

The door was opened to us by a towering butler. He might have been on the skinny side for a troll, but he was taller than the Baron. Little me found him plenty imposing.

'Their Majesties are in the Topaz Parlour,' he informed the Baron.

I had assumed we would have to wait. One did not expect immediate audiences with royals. But to my surprise, Alban led us smartly off into the east wing — doors swinging open by themselves as we approached — and rapped lightly upon an ornately carved door that looked like teak.

'If that is Alban, he may enter,' proclaimed a woman's voice from beyond. I don't use the word "proclaimed" lightly. I swear the voice had its own, ringing echo. She spoke in Court Algatish, which for some reason I am not ignorant of. Considering I had zero expectation of ever attending the Troll Court, why did I learn it? Purely because Farringale and Mandridore are, or were, major centres of learning and there are a lot of lovely old books written in that tongue.

How's that for priorities.

'And he will,' said Alban, and opened the door.

I did not feel prepared, but we were going in. I had time only for a deep breath before I followed the Baron's broad back into a room far too big to deserve the name "parlour". You could have held a feast for thirty people in there. The topaz part was fair enough, though, for pale blue jewels sparkled everywhere: among the floral frieze that ran around the walls, highlighting the patterns embedded in the elaborate plaster ceiling, and glittering from an array of antiques upon the mantelpiece. The walls were painted an exquisite pale jade, matching the silk-and-velvet furniture upholstered in a slightly darker hue.

Amidst all this splendour sat Their Majesties.

Queen Ysurra was a large woman, with the stout figure of a person of sedentary pursuits. Where Baron Alban's skin had a faint bluish cast, hers tended more towards the pale green, as though she, too, had been made to match the room. No court regalia at home; she wore loose silk trousers and a flowing shirt, though the semi-casual effect was somewhat belied by the golden coronet sparkling in her white hair.

King Naldran was a golden creature, his frame still muscular, though his hair was as white as his wife's. He was wearing a dressing gown. An elegant silk confection, to be sure, with ornate braiding and a sumptuous wine-red colour, but it was nonetheless a dressing gown. Oddly, this informality reassured me. We were there for a chat, not an inquisition.

Baron Alban bowed, a little perfunctorily. So did Jay, less so. I gave them my best Milady curtsey.

'Ma'am,' said Alban. 'Sir. Cordelia Vesper, and Jay Patel.'

If you've never been scrutinised by royalty, let me tell you: it is a disconcerting experience. Their Majesties said nothing for rather too long, surveying the pair of us as though they could read our every thought if they only looked hard enough at our faces. For all I knew, perhaps they could.

I tried to think innocent thoughts.

Having considered our attire, Jay's height and my lack thereof, and whatever else they gleaned about us from the staring party, they finally deigned to speak.

'Welcome,' said the queen. 'Thank you for accepting our invitation.'

It had been too official, and perhaps too peremptory, to figure fairly as a mere invitation; it had barely stopped short of a royal summons, perhaps only because we were not technically obliged to obey any such order. But it was a comfortable fiction.

'It is our honour,' I replied, recognising a cue for obsequiousness when I saw one.

Queen Ysurra smiled faintly.

'We wished to extend our personal thanks for your services to our people,' said King Naldran, entirely formal in demeanour despite the dressing-gown. Perhaps he had forgotten he was wearing it.

'That was our pleasure,' said Jay, really getting the hang of the royal interview thing.

'We have need of such bright, active people,' said Ysurra, putting me on my guard. Plebeians flattered the monarchy, not the other way around. Not unless they really, really wanted us for something. And why would they? Mandridore must have been full of clever, efficient folk, perfectly suited for all kinds of shenanigans and chicanery.

The queen glided smoothly on. 'We were most interested to hear of your recent travels abroad, and attendant discoveries. Five Britains at least! What a marvel. And such a Britain, the fifth. It opens up such prospects.'

Aha. They wanted something from Melmidoc's precious, magick-drenched kingdom. Not altogether a surprise. 'It was one of our more entertaining adventures,' I allowed.

'Do you have plans to return?'

What a question. 'Plans, no,' I admitted. 'It is not so easy to travel back and forth between Britains. But hopes... oh, absolutely.'

Queen Ysurra smiled. 'Then perhaps you will be interested in our proposition.'

All right, time to get serious. 'We would be delighted to hear it.'

'We would like to send a delegation into this Fifth Britain,' said the queen. 'It ought, by preference, to consist primarily of those who are best informed, and suitably equipped, to manage both the journey and the assignment with ease.'

I assumed an expression of polite interest.

Queen Ysurra paused, and I thought I detected a hint of uncertainty. She looked at her husband.

King Naldran cleared his throat. 'Few have set foot in this other Britain. Still fewer have ventured into lost Farringale, and know what fate befell it long ago. Is it chance, that there are three in this room who have done both?'

Jay said, his voice a little strained: 'You want us to go back to Farringale.'

The king sat forward. 'Can you imagine what it was like, to lose a place like Farringale? Not the Court. Grandeur may be rebuilt, new palaces raised; all that was lost *there* was bricks and stones and memories. But the history is irreplaceable. The knowledge. The books. All that was there seen and done, all that was discovered and recorded — all lost. And forever. If magick is fading from these shores, the loss of Farringale hastened its demise.

'But now you bring us hope. If there is another, stronger Britain, where magick and its practitioners have lived openly down the years, and enjoyed the freedom to practice and research as they wished, then we must expect they are far more knowledgeable than we. Perhaps they can help us.'

'Just what exactly are you hoping for help with?' I asked, that foreboding feeling flickering to life again.

'We want,' said Queen Ysurra, 'to bring back Farringale.'

3

'*Your* Farringale?' I squeaked. 'The eaten-by-ortherex one?'

Her lips twitched. 'The very one.'

Right. I needed a moment.

See, visiting Farringale was an eye-opening experience. We went there looking for a cure to a disease that was decimating the surviving Troll Enclaves at the time. We found another disease, or more rightly an infestation of all-devouring parasites known as the ortherex. They had, in effect, eaten the population of Farringale alive.

The buildings were still there; the city still stood. But it was an empty shell — one swarmed over by trillions of the repulsive things.

I reminded myself that we were not being asked to revive Farringale ourselves, only to find the means to do so.

'So,' I said, having exchanged a look with Jay. 'You are hoping that someone on the Fifth Britain knows how to get rid of these ortherex beasties.'

'That is our hope,' said Naldran. 'Our good Alban has already consented to undertake the search. Will you oblige us by joining him?'

'Forgive me,' I said, 'but surely you have people enough for such a task. Why employ us?'

'Because,' said the king, and paused. 'Because you seem to have a way with these things.'

I could sort of see his point. It was actually Jay who ended up finding the Fifth first, because he had somehow secured the affections of a perambulatory haunted house. And off she had taken him. I'd found him later, by a separate route. We'd learned a lot about the Britains, and subsequently made it home again — avoiding the memory-wiping enchantment that most of our colleagues (and enemies, among Ancestria Magicka) had been subjected to.

We did have a way of landing on our feet.

What's more, Melmidoc Redclover might even consent to talk to us, and he was the man — sorry, the spriggan — who seemed to know everything.

I looked at Jay again, who stared back, clearly trying to convey something with his eyes.

I had no idea what it was.

'May we have a moment to confer?' I said.

Queen Ysurra inclined her head, exquisitely gracious. 'Please.'

It seemed rude to just walk out, so Jay and I withdrew to a corner.

'What do you think?' I asked him.

'Yes.'

'Yes? Just yes? No ifs, buts, doubts or worries?'

'I have some of all of the above, but so what?'

I blinked at him. 'Are you really Jay?'

'Every inch of me.'

I stared.

'Okay, okay. I know we are probably not supposed to go anywhere near the Fifth again. I know that the Ministry would be unhappy with us if they found out. I know there are risks, and rules. But I want to go back. I always wanted to go back.'

'Me too.'

'Okay then.'

So that was that. We returned to Their Majesties, and the irritatingly smirking Baron (yes, *fine,* Alban, I know our answer was entirely predictable), and gave them to understand that we would be eighty shades of delighted to accept their proposal.

Queen Ysurra actually smiled, a real one. 'How wonderful. If it is agreeable to you, you shall leave in the morning.'

Jay held up a hand. 'Moment. How are we to get there?'

'Is your previous means of travel unavailable?'

'I am not sure. Millie isn't strong, and she needed a couple of days to recover after the last time.'

'It is our hope that she can be persuaded to convey the three of you back to the Fifth. If this does not prove to be the case, then an alternative shall be found for you.'

'Right.'

'Alban has been given a purse of gold for any and all expenses you will naturally incur on this journey,' said the queen. 'I shall further add that we shall be happy to shield you from any... unhappy consequences.'

'As we have already done, on your behalf,' put in the king, referring of course to their having hauled the Ministry's dogs off our backs only a day or two before.

Nice. A reminder that we were already somewhat in their debt — as if we weren't eager enough to go as it was. 'Thanks,' I said, unable to resist the temptation to be a trifle tart.

The Baron tried to smother a laugh, and choked.

'In the meantime,' said the queen, shooting an indecipherable look at her co-monarch, 'the freedom of the Court is yours. In an hour's time we shall appear in state, as is our custom, and the Court will dine. You are welcome to attend.'

The Baron gave me a discreet thumbs-up: *say yes.*

'We'd love to,' I said, needing no prompting whatsoever. An evening of splendour and feasting, at the High Court of the Trolls? They would have the best cooks in the world. A girl would be mad to refuse.

'Then we adjourn,' said the queen, and rose, creaking slightly, from her throne-like chair. 'It is unlikely we will have leisure to confer any further this evening, but any questions that arise may be put to my secretary. He has been instructed to hold himself at your disposal.'

'Thank you,' we said, and set about the business of suitably polite withdrawal.

But the king stopped us. 'One more thing. Perhaps it need not be said, but this is an assignment of the utmost secrecy. We would beg you to keep the matter entirely to yourselves.'

I couldn't even tell Val? How unfair! But one could only promise, which we duly did. He is, after all, the king.

After that we were permitted to exit. We gathered in a knot in the hall, Jay and I buzzing with excitement, the Baron all cool composure as usual.

'I,' I said in sudden, horrified realisation, 'have nothing to wear to a state banquet.'

'I have... something?' said Jay. 'I think?'

'You think?' echoed the Baron. 'If you are not sure, then it most certainly will not do. I shall have to come to your joint rescue.'

I beamed at him. Jay might have scowled. 'The best dress ever?' I said, breathless with hope.

'The *best*, Ves.'

'I might love you a bit.'

His lovely green eyes twinkled down at me. 'Let's hope so.'

AND SO IT WAS that we were introduced to one of the odder quirks of the Court of Mandridore.

One hour later: what was I wearing? It was not the swishy, silky designer dress of my dreams. Let's get that out in the open right away.

Instead of an airy dress of fairy-light gossamer, covered in stars and smelling of roses, I was wearing about half my own bodyweight in fabric. Pale gold silk tissue, to be exact. I had a gown with a long bodice and low waist; enormous, glossy sleeves; a skirt so voluminous, I could've made a pair of sails from the fabric; and delicate lace all around the wide, rather low-cut neckline. My hair was arranged in a thousand ringlets and I had pearls at my throat. I looked like Suzanna Huygens in the Netscher portrait, only rather golder.

Jay had a spectacular cobalt-blue waistcoat covered with embroidery; an even more spectacular coat of pale velvet; knee-breeches and stockings, heeled shoes, and a frothy cravat. Mercifully he had been spared the wig.

See, the loss of Farringale seems to have sunk deeply into the consciousness of the trolls, at least at the new (relatively speaking) Royal Court. And in honour of what was lost, it is customary for everyone to dress like it's still about 1657. I didn't dare ask if they did this all the time.

Accustomed as we are to the freedoms of modern dress, it's no easy matter to step into the fashions of centuries ago. I felt like a ship in full sail, and approximately as unwieldy. But my desire to punch the Baron somewhere painful soon faded, for once I had got used to the sheer volume of my attire (and the weight of it — oof), I began to enjoy it. There is an unabashed frivolity about long-ago Court dress that's rather lacking from modern life. Just look at eighteenth-century hair, if you want an example. In what other era could you have hair three feet high, draped in lace and pearls and crowned with an entire (albeit miniature) sailing ship?

By the time Baron Alban joined us in the hall of the king and queen's mansion, I'd begun to feel quite the princess. He, of course, looked positively princely in crimson velvet, and he'd gone all in on the ribbons.

'You both look perfect,' he informed us.

Jay favoured him with a measured, deeply unimpressed look.

I favoured him with a curtsey. A skirt like that just begs to be gracefully swished as one sinks elegantly into courtly obeisance. (Was I enjoying this a bit too much?)

Alban grinned at me. 'You're a natural. Come on, or we'll be late.'

Outside the mansion, there was no sign of Alban's car. Instead, a pair of coaches had drawn up. They had been plucked straight from a fairy tale, I'd swear it: pale, pretty contraptions, ornately decorated, with sparkling windows and blue velvet inside. Naturally, there were no horses. These were the magickal kind of conveyance.

'No pumpkin coach?' I said to the Baron as he led us to the second of the two. He did not open the door for us himself, as there was a liveried footman to do that. Actually, there were four.

'I tried, but there was a run on them at the last minute and I had to make do with these.'

I shook my head sadly as I got into the coach (utterly gracelessly. I'm not used to being four feet wide from the hip down, and about twice my usual body weight). 'Everyone expects the pumpkin coach treatment these days.'

'I blame Disney. Watch your skirt.' I duly whisked my silken skirts aside as a po-faced footman carefully closed the door on me. Jay joined me on the squishy velvet seat, not nearly so encumbered by his finery as I was by mine. I reflected, not for the first time, on the utter unfairness of historical fashions.

The Baron sat opposite us. 'Now we wait for Their Majesties,' he said, glancing out of the window.

'We're to arrive with them?'

'No. We're to arrive a respectful distance behind them.'

This was better, but not by much. Nor did it make much sense. How were we important enough for such a sign of high favour? They couldn't be that anxious to please us. If we failed at our appointed task, they had a whole Court full of people who'd fall all over themselves to perform any task Their Majesties might set. Surely some of them had the tools to succeed.

I set this puzzle aside for a little later, for once Their Gracious Majesties had been loaded into their own conveyance and trundled off, our coach began to roll, and I devoted my thoughts to mental preparation for the event that lay ahead.

Uppermost among my reflections: *Don't trip on your skirts when you go in, Ves. Just don't.*

4

I DIDN'T, THOUGH JAY tried his level best to do so. We went in together, about two and a half minutes after the king and queen had joined their adoring subjects. Apparently Jay wasn't used to my being four feet wide at the ankles, either, for his foot became tangled in reams of silk and we almost toppled over together.

'Oops,' he said, which about covered it.

I waited while he disentangled himself from my dress. 'I'm a public hazard in this thing.'

'I can't think how there weren't more fatal accidents at the Old Court.'

Let me back up a moment. Their Majesties' private mansion, however fine, had nothing on the real heart of Mandridore: the royal palace. A mere seven or eight minutes in the coach was sufficient to convey us to this spectacular building, and as we waited behind the king and queen's coach I had ample time to get an eyeful of it.

Think Buckingham Palace. Then mentally increase it to about three times the size — not just in width or surface area but in height, too. Unsurprisingly, considering our costumes, the palace was resplendent in the architectural styles of the late sixteen hundreds: square, imposing, symmetrical, and ornate, with arches and pilasters and a splendid cupola.

But there were differences between the palace and the generality of seventeenth-century country house style, chief among them being the minor fact that the entire thing was built out of starstone.

Every last bloody inch of it.

Under the soft light of a rising moon, it positively wallowed in that lovely twilight-blue radiance and I felt sick with something like longing.

Unsure why. Living in a humongous, shiny-blue palace would have its moments, no doubt about that, but it would also get old. Footmen everywhere. Always having to dress for dinner; no slouching about in my old comfies with my hair in a mess. That horrible, echoing sense of loneliness that comes from rattling around in far too much space.

I digress.

They don't do red carpets in troll country, they do gold. All the gold. In Their Majesties swept, prancing elegantly up the gilded carpet as music swelled. We followed shortly after, and I was bemused to note that Their Majesties' courtiers seemed as pleased to see Alban as they were to see the king and queen. I'd underestimated his popularity. Again.

I will skip over the next half hour or so, which passed in a blur of silks and jewels and curtseys and titles. I tried to study the interior architecture but the tumult was too distracting; I received fleeting impressions of painted murals and statuary, rich carpets trampled by a great many feet, and other such Baroque fussiness.

Their Majesties looked around for Baron Alban, more than once. The Baron, inexplicably, chose to remain with us. This held true even at dinner, when I was seated on the Baron's right and Jay upon his left. He talked exclusively to us, which was probably rude of him but I appreciated the thought.

On my other side sat a majestic old troll, his silvery hair elegantly coiffed, his amber velvet coat elaborately decorated.

'You keep high company,' he said to me, nodding at Baron Alban.

'We've worked together a time or two,' I replied, grateful for his kindness in not ignoring me but also wishing he might save the polite chitchat for a bit later. The dining parlour at the palace was twelve miles long and the table several miles longer still, I'd swear. Every inch of it was crowded with dishes, and since one of those nearest to me was a kind of floating pudding consisting of a flock of meringue swans sailing over a lake of sweet cream, my priorities clearly lay elsewhere at that moment.

'I believe I have heard of you,' said my talkative neighbour, ignoring his own plate of fragrant delicacies. 'From the Society for the Preservation of Magickal Heritage, am I correct?'

My mouth being full of cream, I could only nod. It tasted of peaches and rose water.

'I should not repeat gossip, of course, but it is said that you and the young man got as far as Farringale.'

It was not quite a question, but he was watching me with sharp, intent eyes and I realised he was probing for something.

I swallowed my piece of meringue swan-wing. 'It is a true story, though may perhaps have been exaggerated. We barely set foot in Farringale, and saw very little of it.'

My companion clearly wanted to ask more, but the Baron claimed my attention and talked determinedly to me for the next few minutes. By the time I had leisure to glance about again, my amber-clad interlocutor was deep in conversation with his other neighbour.

'Who is that gentleman?' I murmured to Alban.

The Baron spared him one brief, dismissive glance. 'The Marquess of Valony.'

'Surely not,' I blurted.

'He most certainly is,' said Alban, with a raised-eyebrows look at me.

How could I explain my peculiar comment without being insulting? It only struck me as bizarre, that a man enjoying so high a station as marquess should call a mere baron *high company*. Baron was the lowest rank among the aristocracy, at least in my world; a marquess was second only to a duke.

But this was Mandridore, not England. Perhaps things were different here.

After dinner, there was dancing. Delightful, though as soon as I realised I was to take a turn about the ballroom with the Baron, I began to wish that last almond and orange blossom cheesecake uneaten. A mere, weak Ves should never be turned loose upon a banquet like that. It is hazardous to her health.

Fortunately, when the royal orchestra struck up the first strains of music and Their Majesties took to the floor, they chose a slow, stately minuet and I gave a tiny sigh of relief. I would not be obliged to engage in any strenuous gyrations, at least not at present. The king and queen made a handsome couple, though it occurred to me that they looked a little tired as they swept slowly around the centre of the polished marble floor. They were not dancing for the enjoyment of it; they were performing for their subjects. They went through this routine for a few minutes, and then, upon some unheard cue, the floor filled with other couples and Their Majesties withdrew. I wondered if they were obliged to undergo this parade every night. How exhausting.

'I give you fair warning,' I said as the Baron came to claim me. 'I have no idea how to dance a minuet.'

'No one can see your feet anyway.'

'But you can feel them,' I pointed out as he swept me up, and sailed me away on a tide of harpsichords.

'There are advantages to dancing with a featherweight. I shan't even need my steel toe caps.'

I felt a compulsion to correct him on this point, for I am far too fond of food to qualify as the delicate scrap of a thing he described. But compared to him, I suppose I was a mere leaf on the wind.

'I knew there must be some reason you're dancing with me.'

He smiled, just at me. 'Because wit, brains and beauty aren't nearly inducements enough.'

'Flattering,' I murmured, super cool (nobody need know that my heart was turning somersaults). 'But at least half the people here could be described as such, and they're all gagging to dance with you.' Scarcely an exaggeration, that. I was uncomfortably aware that I was attracting a great deal of attention as I whirled about in the Baron's arms. Some of it was merely curious; some of it was outright envious, or something... else. Something else negative.

Alban looked around, as though he hadn't noticed. He didn't look abashed so much as annoyed. 'I knew this was a bad idea,' he muttered.

I felt stricken. 'Dancing with me?'

'No! No. Dancing with you *here.*' His stride faltered, and he pulled me a bit more into his arms, as though to shield me from everyone else. 'Ves, I... ought to tell you something.'

'Ought?'

'I don't want to.'

'Then don't.'

He shook his head. 'If I don't, someone else will. The thing is...' He did not seem to know how to continue, and trailed off.

Jay appeared at my elbow. I'd lost track of him in the ballroom. 'Ves, can I talk to you for a minute?' He made as if to pull me bodily out of the Baron's arms, which was unlike him.

'No,' said Alban, and clutched me closer.

'If you gentlemen think you are going to have a tug of war over me, you are much mistaken,' I said. 'What's the matter, Jay?'

'He's been keeping secrets from you.'

Alban sighed.

'I think he was about to tell me,' I said to Jay.

'He should've told you about six weeks ago.'

I realised that Jay was very angry about something. He looked as composed as ever, but he had an air of suppressed fury I'd never seen before.

'Will somebody tell me what's going on?' I said, hating myself for the plaintive note in my voice.

'Not here,' said Jay. 'Come on. Let's get somewhere quiet.'

But it was not so easy to withdraw from the middle of the dancefloor as all that. Jay tried to escort me out of the thicket of dancers, but they whirled around us in such profusion, we made little progress.

So it was that I was still within hearing distance when a troll matron in a bottle-green gown sang gaily to the Baron as she waltzed past: 'We miss your lady wife tonight, don't we, sir? How long she has been away!'

I stopped dead, to the chagrin of a woman who collided with me mid-minuet. I added her hiss of annoyance to my rapidly growing pile of things-to-ignore, together with the look of mild malice the bottle-green woman had directed at me as she danced away.

I looked at Alban, but none of the thousand questions in my mind made it past my lips.

His broad shoulders sagged. 'Shit,' he said under his breath.

'It's true?' I croaked.

'It— that— I—' He clamped his lips tightly shut and tugged at his perfect hair, a brief gesture of utter dismay. I'd never seen him speechless before. 'That wasn't what I wanted to tell you.'

'It *wasn't*? Were you planning to tell me at all?'

'Yes, I... look, Jay is right, we shouldn't talk here. Come on.'

He swept me away. He had either the bulk or the rank to do it more successfully than Jay, for people melted out of our path. I caught one last glimpse of Jay's enraged face as I was borne away to the far side of the ballroom, and out through an arch onto a starry terrace. The mild summer breeze gently lifted my hair, and I was welcomed by the heady aromas of strawberries and wine.

How romantic.

The Baron escorted me to a bench, but while I sank down upon it in gratitude — my knees might have been shaking a bit — he remained standing. He stood looking down at me with an expression of consternation. 'I'm so sorry,' he said.

'While apologies are nice, I would prefer an explanation.'

He nodded. 'If only it were not so hard to come up with a reasonable one.'

'I'd just like a true one.' I folded my hands together and tried not to stare wistfully at the moonlit sky. I might have been entertaining a few fantasies about being kissed under just such a sky, only quarter of an hour before.

'Jay is right to be angry,' he said with a sigh. 'I never meant to get into this absurd masquerade, only... I never throw rank around when I'm working. It's neither necessary nor helpful. And then, when I decided I liked you, it... it was hard to know how to tell you the truth. The moment never seemed right.'

'Never throw rank?' I repeated. 'But you were introduced as Baron Alban on day one.'

'Yes, but... I am not a baron. Or not only a baron. It's an old title. I am comfortable with it, and it suits the work I generally do for the Court. High enough to open doors, not so high as to be intimidating.'

'High company,' I said, as enlightenment began to dawn.

'What?'

'Just how high in rank are you?'

He ran a hand over his hair again, messing it up. I'd never seen him with disordered hair either. 'I'm a prince,' he said, in the tone a normal person would reserve for something more like *I have syphilis.*

'A prince.'

'*The* prince, actually. I am the next heir to the throne of Mandridore.'

5

BARON ALBAN'S WORDS ECHOED in my mind. *The next heir to the throne of Mandridore.* 'But,' I said, and took a breath. 'But you said— did you *lie?* You said you were not born to eminence.'

'No! I didn't lie. That was true. I am a commoner, same as you. I mean— wait, I didn't mean that.' He gave a great sigh and sank down to the floor, resting his back against the ballroom wall. 'I was given a barony years ago, for services to the Crown. And after that there were a lot more services to the Crown. The rewards piled up. Houses, lands, wealth... for a time, I admit, I was delighted with it all. I'd spent long enough in rootless poverty to appreciate plenty when it came. But it came at a price.

'See, Their Majesties are childless. That's a huge problem for them both personally and... and professionally.

No family, no heir. And the queen's been too old to bear children for some years now. Something had to be done.

'What's less widely known is that she is sick. She's in no imminent danger, but there was no time left to adopt and raise an infant. They needed a capable heir, and fast.

'So they chose me. They knew I could handle the duties of the monarch, I've proved it enough times. And we are... fond of each other.' He stared sightlessly into the middle distance, not looking at me. 'I knew what it would mean if I said yes: nothing about my life would ever be my own again. But how could I refuse? In effect, they were my family already. And they were desperate. So I agreed. That was a year and a half ago.'

He fell silent. 'So you became the crown prince,' I prompted. 'And got married.'

'Some say monarchies are outdated in these modern times, but regardless, they're still here. And they operate according to all the same old rules. The line of succession's been in doubt for long enough. Ysurra wants to see it secure before she dies.

'So they chose a bride for me. Her name is Marit. She's the eldest daughter of the king and queen of Arenmark, the troll kingdom of Norway. She is a good woman.' He paused, and sighed deeply. 'Ice cold, a princess to her fingertips... but I cannot rightly fault her.'

I sat silent, my mind reeling. My jovial, easy-going, occasional colleague Alban was a married crown prince, preparing to take the throne of Mandridore.

In truth, the married part did not altogether surprise me. It had previously entered my head to wonder why so popular a man, with so many obvious advantages, had not been snapped up by some pearl of ladykind long before. Of *course* he wasn't single. What kind of an idiot was I, that I had accepted this apparent incongruity without ever thinking to ask?

But the rest left me reeling.

'Why,' I said after a while, 'were you flirting with me when you're married?'

He looked rather sadly at me. 'Because it is what the old me would have done.'

The old Alban, just a baron and not a prince. Free to explore, free to flirt, free to choose. I watched him for a moment, trying to read his face. I saw mostly sadness. 'Do you regret saying yes to this new life?'

'Sometimes,' he said, so softly I barely heard the word.

Despite my anger and humiliation, I felt a stab of pity for him. He'd trapped himself, and if he was to be believed, he had done it for laudable enough reasons. I tried to imagine the loneliness of the life he had described: married to an as-signed partner, chosen for every advantage but your own. Constantly flattered and courted, but incapable of being truly close to anybody. I could see why he'd enjoyed his interludes with me. It must've been like having a holiday from his new self.

'What was it you were planning to do with me?' In all fairness, I couldn't accuse him of having done anything all that much wrong. He'd flirted, but he hadn't seriously courted me. He'd taken me out to breakfast, but we'd never had a real date. He hadn't even kissed me.

Perhaps it was just my own foolishness that had led me to believe he'd had any of those other things in mind.

'I don't know,' he said dully. 'I just... liked being with you.'

We sat in silence for a while. My thoughts wandered, inconclusively.

Having got over the initial shock, I found I did not hate him. I wasn't even angry. Just a little — a *very* little — disappointed.

'And where is your lady wife?' I said at length.

'In Arenmark. We've met about three times since the wedding.'

'Any children yet?'

'No.'

There was nothing else to say after that, and I didn't try. Small talk would have been unbearable. When Jay finally approached and stood hovering upon the threshold, I was glad enough to rise from my bench, and join him.

'I'd better get to bed,' I said to Alban. 'We should get started early in the morning.'

He nodded, looking at me with his beautiful eyes full of questions. He asked none of them, and I didn't enquire. 'Goodnight, Ves,' was all he said.

'Night, Alban.'

I left him sitting there alone on the balcony, and I hated that I did. One of the things I'd seen in that final glance was the kind of deep, aching loneliness the soul shrinks from acknowledging. I'd wanted badly to stay, and keep him company in whatever fashion I could.

But what good would that do? To him, I could not be any of the things either of us might have wanted. It was going to be difficult enough to forge some kind of working relationship out of this mess.

So I let Jay take me away, grateful for the solicitude that had brought him to my side.

'Are you okay?' he asked as we wove our way to the main doors.

'Fine,' I said firmly. 'Nothing terrible has happened.'

'I'd thought you were becoming fond of him.'

'No comment.'

He smiled faintly. 'Fair enough.' We'd made it out into the corridor by then, which was cooler and mostly deserted. Jay paused. 'You can find your way to your room from here, yes?'

I'd spent an hour in that room not so long ago, dressing and having my hair done. It was a pretty chamber, assigned to me for the night, and I was looking forward to sinking into the enormous canopied bed.

None of this meant I had any idea where in that maze of a palace it was. 'We have met before, haven't we?' I said to Jay, with a look of mock amazement.

He chuckled, and gently took my elbow. 'This way, then.'

UPON THE FOLLOWING MORNING — bright and early, as I had insisted upon — I had occasion to curse my fate in at least one particular.

If I'd had to have my foolish dreams about the baron crushed to death by cold, cruel reality, couldn't it have happened after our important monarch-appointed mission rather than before? For when I arrived at the breakfast-table in our shared parlour, I found Jay and the Baron (no, no, wait. The *prince*) already seated, working their way through plates of pancakes, eggs, bacon and toast in awkward silence. Neither one looked at the other.

'Morning,' I said, sitting a few seats away from them both.

I received attractive smiles from both gentleman, which would've been nice if it hadn't so neatly highlighted the coldness of their treatment of each other. 'Slept well?' said Alban.

'Wonderfully well,' I said with a bright smile. Total lie. I'd slept for about three and a half hours, having taken at least that long to fall asleep. For some reason my head had been spinning too much for repose. I beamed at Jay as well. It was only fair, he being the only one among my present company who hadn't recently fractured my dreams, and applied myself to the nearest dish of pancakes.

I was left with the renewed feeling that there are few disasters that can't be improved upon by a good meal. Once I was suitably filled with excellent pancakes and splendid tea, I felt a lot more equal to the unusual demands of the day.

'So, then,' I said, interrupting the ringing silence. 'We left Millie up at Ashdown. Do we suppose she is still there?'

I was looking mostly at Jay. He had by far the closest relationship with the affable, if mildly deranged, ghost of Millie Makepeace and the rickety old farmhouse she inhabited.

'Probably,' Jay answered, pushing an abandoned piece of strawberry around his plate with his fork. 'She ought not to have recovered the strength for another jump yet.'

I wondered what was eating Jay. He looked positively woebegone, one elbow planted on the table and his chin in his hand. I couldn't see why the news of the Baron's true circumstances would affect him all that much, and he'd had all night to get over his anger on my account. 'So we'll go back there.' I turned to Alban. 'Is there a Waypoint somewhere here that we can use?'

'Of course.' He abandoned his own plate, still mostly full, and rose from the table. 'It's at our disposal whenever we wish.'

'Then we'd better not waste any time.' I rose as well, casting a last, regretful look at the leftover pancakes. 'Jay?'

He'd seemed lost in thought, but he looked up at the sound of his name. 'Hmm?'

'I've just volunteered you to Waymasterify us back to Ashdown. Or as near it as possible.'

'Right.' He blinked a couple of times, visibly pulling his thoughts back from parts unknowable, and made for the door.

I stayed behind a moment with Alban. 'Listen, if we can forget about last night for the next few days, I think that would be best. We need to focus on work.'

He nodded. 'I would like nothing better myself.'

I nodded too, smiling around the unaccountable sinking of my stupid heart. 'Great. I'll see you in a few minutes. I just need to fetch my stuff.'

Back in my room, I found the pup was (for once) awake. She came running to greet me as I opened the door, her puff of a tail wagging furiously. She practically vibrated with joy, and I bent to pet her, feeling a little soothed. 'Hi, Puppins.'

My good feelings waned a bit when I saw what she had done with every item of value in the room. They were piled in a heap in the middle of my lovely four-poster bed, wound up in the blankets in a neat nest.

'You are a menace,' I informed her sternly, her only response to which was to yip cheerfully at me and grin. 'This,' I said, brandishing my string of pearls at her, 'is not yours! Nor is it mine! How would I explain it to Their Majesties if we walked off with — or *broke* — all these jewels and antiques?' For she had been most industrious. Everything from ivory figurines to ear-jewels lay nestled together among her haul.

We had a short wrestling match as she tried to reclaim the treasures I was rapidly divesting her of. Being, for once, the bigger, stronger party, I won.

She curled up at the foot of the bed and stared at me with huge, mournful eyes.

'I know,' I muttered. 'Life's a bitch, isn't it?'

6

The grounds of Ashdown Castle were beautiful, once.

Then we'd happened.

Actually, to be fair, Fenella Beaumont had happened. It was she who had enslaved several hapless Waymaster spirits and forced them to jaunt off with the castle. We'd obliged the castle's inhabitants to come back without it, Fenella included — leaving the building itself camped on the shores of Whitmore Isle on the Fifth Britain. Zareen and George were out there somewhere, too.

We would be more unpopular with Ancestria Magicka than ever, should they recover their memories of these thrilling events.

When Jay, Alban and I arrived at Ashdown we found a mess of dark, ruined earth where the castle once stood.

Only a few outbuildings lingered: the stable block, and assorted others, most of them in ruins. There was no sign of Fenella, or of any of the rest of her organisation. I wondered where, in their confusion, they might have chosen to decamp to.

More unfortunately for us, we found no sign of Millie Makepeace, either.

She's hard to miss. Big, craggy and built from flint, she is a farmhouse somewhere north of two hundred years old. A bit shabby around the edges, perhaps; some of her stones are falling out, and her doors and window-frames are in need of a fresh coat of paint. She also has a habit of singing. Loudly.

But the burgeoning sunlight of early morning shone dewily down upon an empty, silent space, an occasional old oak swaying gently in the breeze.

'Setback,' I said, turning in a circle to survey the grounds in their entirety. Nothing.

'Millie!' Jay called. The word echoed hollowly over the ragged, grassy ground and no reply came.

The spirit of Mellicent Makepeace had brought the lot of us back — all of Fenella's dinner guests squashed into a house that, though large as such buildings went, could barely accommodate so many. We'd beat a hasty retreat after that, and had not stayed to see what became of the house.

'Where might a dispossessed farmhouse with homicidal tendencies go when she's tired?' I asked.

'Wherever Ancestria Magicka told her to, probably,' said Jay. 'I tried to tell her she shouldn't listen to that lot, but I don't think she was hearing me.'

I felt a moment's compunction on Millie's account. We ought to have taken better care what happened to her. Only we'd been exhausted at the time, confused and disoriented ourselves, and urgently in need of returning Home and reporting to Milady. And Millie came off as a woman/house who could take care of herself.

'Shh!' said Jay suddenly, and froze.

I waited.

'Do you hear that?'

I didn't — and then I did. A distant, thin sound, like an eerie wail. Then another.

A few seconds later, she was hitting the high notes. I winced.

'Come on.' Jay set off in the general direction of the singing. Alban and I, without looking at each other, followed.

We found Millie parked on the very edge of the Ashdown property, as though she'd been making a bid for freedom and then lacked the energy to take the final step. Huddled in the midst of a circle of ancient elms, she sat swaying slightly from side to side, her stones rumbling, and singing some wordless song of woe.

Her front door was missing, and by the looks of it, someone had taken an axe to her porch-fence and windows. Shattered glass lay everywhere.

'Millie!' hollered Jay, for the third time. 'Mellicent Makepeace!'

The house stopped wailing. *Mr. Patel?*

Jay, looking furious again, stomped in through the empty space where her front door had been. 'What's happened to you?'

She did! said Millie tragically. *She did not know what she was doing here without her castle, but said that it must be my fault somehow.*

She was presumably Fenella Beaumont. I winced, my guilt deepening. It had not occurred to me that, in the absence of an obvious culprit for the ruin of her plans (me, Jay and the Society in general) the woman might turn on Millie.

Jay sighed, and awkwardly patted her ruined door frame. 'I'm sorry. We'll get you a new door.'

'And windows,' I added, following Jay inside. 'I'm sure such things can be arranged for on Whitmore.'

'How about that, Millie?' said Jay. 'Do you want to get out of here?'

Yes! she hissed. *And I am never, ever, ever coming back.'*

There followed the sounds of muffled sobbing.

'Fenella really needs to work on her staff satisfaction,' I muttered. So the leader of Ancestria Magicka had a temper. Usefully possessed houses like this one were not in plentiful supply; she must have been absolutely incensed to treat Millie so cruelly. It was, to say the least, unwise.

I smiled, and leaned against her parlour wall in what I hoped was a comforting manner. 'May we offer you alternative employment with the Society? Absolutely no axes, ever. All the doors and windows you'd like. And you'd be near Jay all the time.'

Jay shot me an appalled look.

Jay? said Millie. *You mean Mr. Patel?*

'That's right.'

A moment's silence. Then: *And who is this gentleman?* said Millie, in a tone I could only describe as caressing.

Baron — *Prince* Alban — had kept his own counsel up until then, and taken up a station in a quiet corner, observing the proceedings in a silence I hoped was only thoughtful, not grim. He looked up at that, his eyes almost as wide as Jay's. 'Er,' he said, with uncharacteristic hesitation. 'My name's Alban, Miss Makepeace.'

The temperature in the house, previously frigid, warmed a perceptible few degrees. *And do you work for the Society also, Mr. Alban?*

I shot his highness a warning look.

'Er, yes,' he said. 'For the time being.'

Excellent, she crooned. *Then I accept. What are to be my duties?*

I looked at Jay to see how he'd taken the defection of his loyal sycophant. He was smiling.

I suppose the dog-like devotion of a lugubrious, murdering deadwoman would grow wearisome.

'Conveyance,' said Jay. 'We'd like to go back to that nice island you took me to before. Do you think you're feeling up to it?'

Am I up to it! Millie's incorporeal voice rang with enthusiasm. *Just try to stop me!*

'Wait a moment, I—' began Jay, but too late, for Millie's timbers were already shivering (so to speak) and a wave of energy shot from floor to ceiling, setting my teeth on edge.

With a *whoosh,* we were gone.

Three minutes later, my bones still vibrating from the journey, I stepped out of Millie's front porch, eager to catch another glimpse of lovely, exciting Whitmore.

What met my eye absolutely was not that.

'Miss Makepeace?' I ventured. 'I think we've missed Whitmore.'

Jay and Alban joined me on the porch. We stared in silence at the view: an expanse of featureless land, largely desolate, with no trees, buildings or other prominent structures. The terrain was lumpy, dull and muddy, with a desultory smattering of rough, colourless grass. As flat as Lincolnshire, with a drab, stony beach tacked on at the edge, it gave way in the distance to a steel-grey sea. A thick mist hung in the air, obscuring what, if anything, lay beyond the water.

This is Whitmore, said Millie crossly. *I am sure of it.*

'Different Whitmore,' said Jay briefly.

'Did this happen before?' I asked.

'No. But there are several Britains, and we didn't specify which one we wanted.'

'You said "the nice island we went to before."'

'She's tired,' said Jay pacifically.

'Tired?' I said in a low voice. 'Or untrustworthy?'

Jay raised his voice. 'Millie, you weren't told to bring us here, were you?'

I rolled my eyes. 'Subtle.' If it was May on that particular Britain, there was no sign of it. The wind was chilly, the air damp, and my optimistically thin summer dress was not up to the demands of the weather. I began to shiver.

You were not supposed to guess that, said Millie in a small voice. *They said you would never ask.*

All right, I stood corrected. Subtlety wasn't always superior.

'They?' prompted Jay. 'You mean Fenella?'

Who's that?

'The bitch with the axe,' I supplied.

Yes. With a subdued roar of loose stonework, the house began to tremble. *She said they would demolish me if I did not do as they asked.*

Alban said mildly, 'You might like to stop being a building?'

THIS IS MY HOUSE. Millie's voice thundered through my bones.

Alban swallowed. 'All right.'

This turn of events bothered me, for it suggested that Fenella's memories of the past day or so were only patchy, not altogether erased. She remembered the several Britains; well, naturally enough. She must have known about them for a long time. But she also remembered that we had been involved in the wreck of her plans, and apparently had vindictiveness enough to want to take revenge.

Tiresome woman.

'Millie,' Jay was saying. 'You're with us now, remember? You don't need to keep us here.'

She will demolish me.

'She will not. We won't let her get anywhere near you.'

I tried to remember what Melmidoc had said. A couple of the nine known Britains were gone (and now was not a good time to think too hard about how that had come about). Actually, hadn't he said three? So that left six. The Whitmore of our own Britain (the sixth) had sunk, so that wasn't it either. And if we weren't on the fifth, that left four possibilities: the two where magick had been out-lawed, or the two where magick had died out altogether.

'So we are either breaking the sacred law of the land,' I said out loud, 'or we've become the local equivalent of flying pigs and will probably be put in a museum.'

'By whom?' said Alban, and made a show of looking around at the general desolation.

Excellent point.

'Millie,' I said more loudly. 'Did I mention that Mr. Alban is a prince?'

I received a filthy look from the erstwhile Baron, but I achieved my immediate object: Millie's litany of complaints stopped abruptly. *A real one?*

'One hundred percent authentic. And the prince is on an urgent royal mission, to the other Whitmore. The one where Melmidoc lives. You are in the service of a future king, Miss Makepeace.'

See, royalty has an odd way of impressing people. It's true today, and I was gambling on the likelihood that it was still more true a couple of centuries ago. Back then, aristocrats and royals really did own the world.

Millie hesitated. *But the bitch with the axe—*

'Is no match for a royal prince.' I winked at Alban, who perceptibly winced.

But then he took another long look at the featureless landscape we were stranded in, and sighed. 'How would you like to be an official royal residence, Miss Makepeace?'

The flint stones began to rumble again, but this time with excitement. *Royal?* Millie squeaked. *Me?*

'The Court is in need of a more, ah, informal establishment. Not too informal, of course,' he added, as Millie began to object. 'I can see a few silk carpets in your future; some velvet drapes; maybe a chaise longue...'

'And,' I put in firmly, 'no one will dare to demolish a royal residence, will they?'

Fenella was unlikely to be deterred by such trivialities, of course, but Millie need not know that. My real plan was to make sure (if at all possible) that Fenella never got anywhere near the farmhouse ever again.

She was ours, now.

There was something endearingly deranged about Miss Makepeace. Those lightning changes of mood, for one, from woebegone to effervescent. *I am at your service, Your Highness!* the house breathed.

I mentally apologised to Alban for lumbering him with Millie's lonely heart. No part of me was motivated by irritation at his partial capture of mine, I swear. Desperate times. Needs must.

He'd missed his cue. The silence stretched, and I was obliged to nudge him with my toe. Or kick him. It might have been more of a kick.

'Wonderful,' sighed Alban. 'Then, Miss Makepeace, pray take us to Melmidoc's Whitmore on the fifth Britain.'

Right away, Your Highness!

'Carefully—' yelped Alban, to no avail. With a great, shuddering *whoosh* and an unpromising tearing sound, Millie hauled the lot of us off.

7

WHITMORE IS A CENTRE of learning, Melmidoc had said. He had banged on a bit about this point, smugly self-satisfied about all the academics (even from our Britain!) who flocked to the Centre of Government for the North on the fifth Britain. Not only politically effective but scholastically, too. Lovely. Excellent.

Only, when Miss Makepeace pulled up on the cliff-top over the sea for our second visit there, it did not much resemble either of those things.

The first thing that attracted our notice was the music. It pulsed through the floor, a thumping beat reverberating through Millie's crumbly old walls, and somewhere out there was a large crowd of people raucously singing.

Millie approved. I gathered this from the way she immediately began singing along.

I didn't, so much.

Crunch them, punch them, bash their faces in! sang Millie, bouncing along to the beat.

Jay, Alban and I decided in unison to exit stage left. We erupted out of the house at a run, and having put a safe distance between ourselves and the wildly gyrating farmhouse, we stood in momentary, flabbergasted silence.

'Those aren't really the lyrics, are they?' I said after a while. The general tumult made it pretty hard to tell.

'I don't think it's English,' said Alban.

Leave it to Millie not only to make up her own lyrics, but to go all in for violence while she was at it. I began to question the wisdom of having forged an alliance with that one.

'So, party's on,' said Jay, looking around.

'You reckon?' Millie had taken us to the end of the same street we'd run down (a couple of times) a few days before. Apparently it was her favourite spot to loiter in. But the other houses in the row were different today. As mismatched as before — higgledy-piggledy thatched-roof cottages rubbing elbows with elegant starstone properties — they were all decked alike in colourful bunting. This being Whitmore, the bunting did not hang limply against the whitewashed or bluish-stone walls, as they would in our Britain. The bunting floated up there by itself, and it wiggled and bopped along to the beat with as much enthusiasm as Millie.

So did the cottages.

'Oh, lord,' I sighed. I mean, I'm a sucker for life and colour and music, I really am. But when literally nothing around you is standing still, the effect quickly becomes dizzying.

I put my hands over my eyes.

'There's the spire,' said Jay. I dared to uncover my eyes, only to see, when I followed the line of Jay's pointing finger, Melmidoc's spire enthroned at the highest point of the island, swaying from side to side.

'They really like their music out here,' I muttered.

Jay was getting into it. I knew this because he was bopping, too. 'It's like being on a boat,' he said, catching my eye. 'Try too hard to act like you're on normal ground and you'll probably fall over. But when you learn to go with the flow...'

I gave an experimental bop. 'You know, Jay, I think you were made for this place.'

'Told you I wanted to stay.'

Alban had wandered off in the direction of the spire, threading his way through the singing people with surprising ease given his size. Then again perhaps it was because of his size; when Jay and I followed, we frequently found ourselves boxed in, blocked or pushed. I quickly abandoned politeness in favour of pushing back, making full use of my elbows. Jay looked a bit shocked, but he's never been five-foot-not-much. You do what you must. I kept one hand clamped firmly over my shoulder bag en route; the last thing we needed just then was for my over-excitable pup to bounce out and dash away. I'd never find her again.

By the time we finally caught up with Alban, we found him leaning casually against the spire, arms folded, surveying the partying Whitmore with an expression of faint bemusement. I hoped it might have put the twinkle back in his eyes, but I hoped in vain. 'And I thought the Court had a talent for dissipation,' he said. It was a creditable attempt at his old humour, even if his smile was crooked.

'If only Westminster would take a leaf out of Whitmore's book,' I said, smiling back. 'Parliamentary debates would be so much more interesting.'

Back already? came Melmidoc's voice, at a thundering volume. The tall, narrow door of the pale spire rattled in its frame, and then sprang open with a hollow *boom*.

'I still haven't figured out how to world-hop,' said Jay. 'I need more practice.'

World-hop?

Some of our modern terminology escaped Melmidoc, perhaps especially when we were being sarky.

'Jump from Britain to Britain,' Jay explained. 'You did say you'd teach me?'

I did, Melmidoc allowed. *But that was before a hundred more of you appeared.*

'They're all gone,' Jay said quickly. 'It's just the three of us.'

You were supposed to be amnesiated.

Jay coughed. 'We… sort of were…'

I judged it a good moment to interrupt. 'What's going on here today? With the music, and everything?'

It is the Feast of Delunia! The most important festival of the magickal year, marked by a full week of celebration.

I swallowed my dismay at the word *week*. 'And what is being commemorated?'

The spire consented to stop swaying for a moment, though I felt a faint tremor in the floor that ran in time with the beat. Melmidoc was, in effect, tapping his feet. *In the dark ages of the later seventeenth century there were those who feared magick. The result was a growing movement to ban it, which is precisely what happened in certain other, lost Britains. Delunia was one of the greatest sorceresses who ever lived, and a talented politician besides. Thanks to her diligence and dedication, these motions were never passed, and instead of dying out, magick went thereafter from strength to strength. She faced great personal danger in order to do it, too, for some called for her to be burned — indeed, she almost was! Without her, the fifth Britain would not be as you see it today.* He gave a windy sigh, and added wistfully: *She was beautiful, too.*

'Is there feasting as well as music?' said Alban.

Every imaginable delicacy! Melmidoc uttered these words with an enthusiasm for food that might even rival mine. Could a building imbibe comestibles? I wasn't sure I wanted to think about it.

Alban grinned at me. 'Does that reconcile you to a week of tumult, Ves?'

'It just might,' I conceded.

'Course,' said Alban, straightening his face. 'We are here to work.'

'Serious work,' I agreed. 'Zero dancing.'

'Little bit of feasting.'

'Little bit. Melmidoc, we've come to pick your brains.'

I shall teach the little Waymaster, he announced. *After the party.*

Jay looked torn between delight at the concession and affront at the word "little". 'Thanks,' he managed.

Hey, welcome to my world.

'That's completely wonderful,' I said. 'But actually we're here about something else.'

Jay trod on my foot.

'As well!' I yelped. 'Something else *as well as* the Waymaster training.'

I shall be intrigued to hear it, said Melmidoc, in a voice that suggested otherwise.

'It is nothing onerous.'

'Hopefully,' put in Alban.

'Hopefully it's nothing onerous. Melmidoc, is there — or was there — a Farringale here?' I didn't feel the need to explain about Farringale to him. The Redclover brothers hadn't disappeared from our Britain until around 1630. At that time, Farringale was still the most powerful Fae Court in the land; it hadn't begun to decline until nearly thirty years later. Indeed, Melmidoc had undergone a few battles with the monarchs of Farringale himself.

Was? he echoed blankly. *Is there not a Farringale every-where?*

Interesting. 'There *was* a Farringale in our Britain, but it's gone now.'

'Not quite gone,' corrected Alban. 'The city is still there, even if it is empty.'

Empty? Melmidoc didn't speak for a while. Then he said, sharply, *What became of the Court?*

So we explained: about the sudden, hurtling decline of Farringale after Melmidoc had vanished into the fifth Britain; about the move to Mandridore; about our own visit into what was left of Farringale, and what we had found there. About the ortherex parasites who had swallowed the city whole, and the few sentinels from the Old

Court who had, at great personal cost, lingered as fading guardians ever since.

It made for a splendid, if heart-breaking tale.

Even Melmidoc seemed to feel it so, for all his resentments over past troubles. The spire ceased to sway, and I'd swear the music receded more and more as we talked, as though he was muting it to match his own feelings.

The brutality of time, he said, once we had finished our tale. *So much is lost.*

'That's literally what our entire job is about,' I agreed. 'Trying to salvage what is left of magick before we lose the lot. That being the case, this assignment is highly interesting. It isn't often we have the option of bringing something back.'

'*If* we do,' Alban said. 'It's a dream.'

'Dreams come true sometimes.' I smiled at him, but he did not smile back.

The ortherex, said Melmidoc, and stopped. He was silent for a while, perhaps thinking. *What do you know of those creatures?*

'They feed primarily upon troll-kind,' I said. 'Not their flesh, exactly. They lay eggs in living troll-flesh and the growing parasites feed off the magickal energies of the host, draining them dry. Usually, the troll dies.'

'They can be countered,' put in Jay. 'To some degree. We brought a cure out of Farringale, or the recipe for one. It treats the effects of ortherex-infestation, though I think the poor sod still has to be operated upon to remove the eggs. Many sufferers have been saved, since.'

I would be interested to learn of this recipe, Melmidoc said. *The ortherex are a persistent problem in this magick-drenched Britain, and they do not limit themselves to troll hosts alone.*

'Mauf probably has it,' I offered.

Mauf?

'My cursed book.' I rummaged in my shoulder bag. We'd moved inside the spire by then, so I closed the door and let the pup out. She stretched, yawned hugely, and tottered off to explore. I was pleased to see a dish of water and a matching dish of meat appear at the bottom of the stairs. Melmidoc was used to the Dappledok pups.

I drew Mauf out, showing off his handsome purple binding. 'But if the ortherex are such a problem, does that mean you have no way to destroy them?'

They are like any pest or parasite. They breed at incredible speed. To eradicate them entirely must be an impossible dream.

I was crestfallen to hear that; my hopes of a speedy solution to the problem evaporated. 'Do you have any way of combating them? Anything that might help to clear Farringale?'

I believe you are asking the wrong questions, said Melmi-doc.

I paused in the process of opening Mauf's cover. 'I beg your pardon?'

The pertinent question is not: how to remove the ortherex. The question must be: why are they still there? If the city is empty as you say, and has remained so for centuries: on what are they feeding? If they need live hosts in which to lay their eggs, how is it that they are breeding?

Jay and I exchanged a look that said: *We are the biggest idiots currently breathing.*

Alban, however, seemed electrified. 'You're right. They should have died off long ago.'

Indeed. Let us consider, then. Perhaps there is no way to destroy them, but an alternative solution is to remove whatever is keeping them alive.

8

'YOU SAID THE ORTHEREX of this Britain are stronger,' I said to Melmidoc. 'And they don't confine themselves to just troll hosts. What else do they like?'

All of the more distinctly magickal races have suffered their share of infestations, Melmidoc replied. Though, interestingly, it is only sentient creatures who are afflicted. There have been no recorded cases of ortherex feeding upon, or breeding within, any species of magickal beast.

That eliminated my first theory. The only other living creatures we had encountered at Farringale were griffins. While they were splendidly magickal, I did not think they were sentient.

Probably.

'Mauf, are griffins—' I began, opening the rich purple cover of my precious book. But there I stopped, for I'd received an eyeful of his title page. '....That's new,' I observed.

'In point of fact,' said Mauf loftily, 'It is a very old technique.'

'I know that, but I've never seen you employ it before.'

'I understand my predecessor to have been stolen, once. I humbly suggest that he would not have been, had he taken the correct precautions.'

'Like this one, for example?'

'Precisely like this one.'

I read the title page aloud. 'Whoever steals this book, may they be drowned in water. And if they be not drowned in water, may they be burned in fire. And if they be not burned in fire, may they be hanged from the neck. And if they be not hanged from the neck, may they ingest poison. And if they do not ingest poison, may they be eaten by wolves. And if they be not eaten by wolves, may they fall from a great height. And if they do not fall from a great height...' I turned the page and stopped reading, for it went on. And on.

'Taking no chances, eh, Mauf?' said Jay.

I patted the book gently. 'Maufry, you do know that medieval thief-curses don't work?'

'Who says that they do not?'

The practice had persisted in some quarters well past the medieval era, in fact, for the belief in their efficacy as curses had endured. It had taken a large study, sponsored by the Hidden Ministry in its earlier days, to establish that many were fake. Or not so much fake as insufficient; they were just words, usually written down by those who had no magick. A real thief-curse needed no words, and since the authentic kind were genuinely deadly, they had, of course, been banned by the Ministry long ago.

But Mauf was bristling in my hands, and the tone of his dusty book-voice was both defensive and slightly injured. So I said, 'Never mind,' and weakly changed the subject. 'Ortherex, Mauf. I am sure you must know a lot about those.'

'Having sat helpless upon my shelf while they ate up my city around me, I can say with some justification that I do.'

'What did they do?'

'They drank up the magick of Farringale and dined upon its inhabitants, until the population lay dead in droves.'

'And then what?'

'I do not know, Miss Vesper. I, like my fellow tomes, fell deeply into slumber. What was left to wake for?'

'Wait,' said Jay, frowning. 'We were there. We saw empty streets, quite clean. It was nothing like Darrowdale. If the people all died, why didn't we see bones? Skeletons?'

'Did they *all* die?' said Alban. 'Some fled, and founded Mandridore.'

'And stuck around long enough to clean up the streets before they left? With the place infested with ortherex, and the threat of catching the infection any moment?'

He was right; that didn't make sense.

I was silent, for another question was swirling about in my mind. If the parasites existed still in the fifth Britain, and had in fact grown stronger down the ages... why had there been no Farringale incident here? Why were they still accounted only as pests, not as disasters?

How was it that the things had suddenly grown so all-powerful in the 1650s as to wipe out Farringale within a year?

I was beginning to realise that this was in no way normal.

I relayed these thoughts, and Alban's frown deepened. 'Their Majesties believe it to have been something along the lines of a natural disaster,' he said. 'Tragic, but no more preventable than a hurricane or a volcanic eruption. Perhaps they're wrong.'

'If so, this could be a lot more complicated than simply clearing out the ortherex,' said Jay. 'We need to make sure they stay gone — and that means we need to know how they got there in the first place, and how they proliferated so fast.'

Maybe Their Majesties had more of an inkling than Alban suspected, for had I not asked myself why they had involved Jay and me? We were human. The ortherex of our Britain left humans alone, or so Baroness Tremayne had said. The king and queen couldn't send people like Alban back into Farringale; they would be in terrible danger. But the Society's members mostly weren't trolls. Were we to be sent back to Farringale, once we'd found the way to fight the ortherex? I felt a flicker of excitement at the idea. This was hero-tale stuff.

Anyway. Focus. Answers first, heroics later. 'Alban,' I said. 'How much is known of Farringale's history directly before its demise?'

'Not as much as you'd think. Those who fled the city salvaged what they could, but they were fleeing for their lives. It wasn't all that much. Most of the library was left behind, as you saw, and those who founded Mandridore weren't necessarily scholars. They were too busy building the new Court to produce detailed accounts of what they'd left behind them, or so we assume. It's a hazy period.'

'I am beginning to wonder if there wasn't something else going on,' I said. 'Did the Court have enemies?'

'It was a supremely powerful Court. Of course it had enemies.'

'Any among rival powers?'

Alban looked thoughtfully at me. 'Interesting question, Ves.'

'Those were brutal times. The non-magickal folk were chopping the heads off their own kings. Who's to say what the Fae Courts might have been doing to one another?'

'Interesting, hideous question, Ves.'

'Where can we go to get more answers?' I said. 'Mel, you implied there is a Farringale in this Britain.'

Mel. How charmingly brief.

I'd heard the dragon, Archibaldo, address Melmidoc as "Mel," but perhaps I had not yet earned that right. Fair.

'Mr. Redclover,' I amended.

The air rippled with amusement. *It is indeed the case that Farringale reigns on over the fifth.*

'And is it still a centre of learning?'

Some even believe that it rivals Whitmore as such.

Melmidoc obviously disagreed.

'What have you got here?' interjected Jay. 'Anything good on the ortherex?'

After a short silence, Melmidoc said: *I do not recall that the scholars of Whitmore have made a specialty of the study, but I am certain something can be found to interest you.*

I tapped Mauf's gold-edged pages. 'Anything to add, Mauf?'

'Not a great deal, Miss Vesper.'

I should like to borrow that book.

'What?' I said, surprised. 'Mauf?'

It is a highly interesting piece of work.

'It?' said Mauf. 'I am a gentleman, sir.' His front cover snapped crisply shut, sending a puff of dust flying out from… somewhere.

Precisely my point.

'If Mauf does not object, I am sure you may have an audience with him,' I offered.

I shall be very much obliged.

Mauf maintained an offended silence for a few seconds, but flattery has ever worked wonders upon his vain little heart. 'Oh, very well,' he said huffily. 'If Miss Vesper would like me to have conversation with this ghost, I shall, as always, be delighted to please her.'

I'll here own up that flattery works wonders upon my vain little heart, too. I smiled.

'However uncouth he may be,' added Mauf.

I smirked. 'You two will get along splendidly.'

The main problem with Whitmore as a prominent centre of learning is that it is rather small. Being already the Centre of Government for the North, or whatever Mel had called it, as well as the home of a reasonably thriving population of scholars, sorcerers and assorted others, there is already a lot to make room for. By the time you've added in a smattering of classrooms, magickal laboratories and lecture halls, that's about it for space.

As such, the library to which we were later escorted was dishearteningly compact. Scarcely larger than the library at Home, in fact. Which was not to disparage it too much; Val's library is a wonderful resource, one which has come to my aid many a time. Only, when one is looking for detailed knowledge upon a specialist, if not outright esoteric, subject, one hopes for a certain breadth.

I'd left Mauf lounging at the spire, giving Melmidoc a hard time. The pup, however, came along with us. I thought she was in sore need of some exercise, and perhaps a bit of social time with some others of her own kind. Mel assured us she would not wander off for long; they were loyal, the Dappledok pups. Nonetheless, I'd suffered a twinge of anxiety as we left the spire, for the pup had bombed straight past us and disappeared up the street at a gallop, ears and tail flying. We hadn't seen her since.

The music had met us with a roar as we'd made our way to the library Mel described, and I'd spared a hope that it would be as muted among the books as it had been inside Melmidoc's spire. I love music, but it is no easy task to study through someone else's ear-shattering party.

The library, as it turned out, was everything I could have wished for. Almost eerily silent, with a web of complex enchantments to block out all sound from beyond the walls; stuffed floor to ceiling with books, making the most of every available inch of space; and, considering that it was party season, encouragingly deserted. I do so enjoy having a library to myself.

Well, not quite to myself, but I did not mind sharing with Jay and Alban.

We were met by the librarian on duty. Sort of.

When I said they were making the most of every possible inch, I mean that their attitude to space was a little different to ours. On our Britain, we need things like walls to support bookcases, and floors upon which to stand desks and chairs. On the fifth, apparently they do not. The librarian sat at a heavy oak desk floating some eight feet above our heads, surrounded by a small fleet of other such furniture. She reached for a book as I watched, and plucked it from a shelf tucked just under the ceiling. Well, why bother clambering up ladders to fetch the books down when you can go up to meet them? It was like my flying chair trick, only about ten times more powerful.

A deep lust uncurled in my covetous soul, and I suddenly had no trouble understanding why Jay had been reluctant to leave.

So absorbed was the librarian in her work, whatever it was, that she did not notice our entry. At length, Jay discovered a bell hovering near the door, and lightly rang it.

'Oh!' said she, peering down at us. 'Just a moment. Sorry.'

"A moment" turned out to be more like three or four minutes, but at last she drifted down — her chair did, anyway, with her seated upon it; the desk remained up near the ceiling. She smiled at us and said: 'I wasn't expecting anybody today.'

Justifiably enough; the people of Whitmore really knew how to party. 'We're visiting,' I told her. Her appearance fascinated me a little. She was as short as me, but thinner, even fragile-looking, with pale, wispy hair and sea-green eyes. Human enough, I thought, but not human through-and-through; her features, her air of ethereal delicacy, suggested to me that she had significant fae heritage somewhere in her family tree. Was that common for Whitmore? Or perhaps across the whole of the fifth? Perhaps it was. If the magick half of the world had no need to hide themselves, it stood to reason that intermingling would lead to more people of mixed heritage.

I liked this.

'Melmidoc sent us down here,' Jay told her, which wasn't a bad move. 'We're looking for anything you have on ortherex infestations.'

Her face lit up at mention of Melmidoc's name — and then fell again at Jay's next words. Hardly surprising. Could there be a more deeply unsexy subject than pest management?

'Our focus tends to be on more arcane subjects, but I'll see what I can find.' She went off, on foot this time, to consult an enormous tome chained to a pedestal some way behind her. An old-school library catalogue, a foot thick, its spine supported by chunky bronze hinges and its pages clad in thick green leather. Did they not have computers on Whitmore? Not that I was displeased. My nerdy little soul blazed with delight at sight of so beautiful a book.

I heard a cheery yip from behind me, and whirled. There was my pup!

...and at least twenty others. They came streaming in the library door, tails waving like flags, noses scooting along the ground as they scattered everywhere.

'Oops,' said Jay. 'Maybe should not have left the door open.'

'Um.' I eyed the wriggling yellow furries doubtfully. 'Which one of you is Pup?'

'You still haven't given her a name?' said Alban, and then pointed out one of the pups — the one presently trying to climb the leg of the nearest desk. 'There she is.'

'How can you tell?'

'She's got your ring on her horn.'

She did, too. My right ring finger was bare of the labradorite hoop that usually adorned it. The jewel lay instead around the base of my disgraceful pup's single horn, a glint of pearly rainbow colours among her yellow fur.

'How did you—?!' I resisted the temptation to clutch at my golden hair, the colour of which could not be changed without that ring, and set off after her.

'How about Robin Goodfellow?' Alban called after me.

9

LATER, HAVING PEELED Ms. Goodfellow off the leg of
the desk, pried my Curiosity out of her possession, and
ushered her legion of new friends out of the door again
(social butterfly, my pup), we were presented with one,
meagre book by our new librarian friend. It was a thin
thing, with anaemic white covers and a disappointing lack
of heft.

'It's really not a popular topic,' said the librarian, no
doubt meaning to be kind as she demolished our mission
in a mere six words.

I leafed through it. It contained annotated diagrams of
an ortherex parasite and its eggs and larva, plus some notes
as to its preferred habitats (rocky spaces in adulthood,
especially underground, and a warm, magickal body for
the eggs). Young and old alike fed greedily off magickal

energies, the fresher the better, which is why they tended to collect in Dells, Dales and Enclaves.

Speaking of which. 'Farringale is still an active Dell, isn't it?' I said aloud.

'You mean in the magickal sense?' asked Alban. 'It seemed to be. It's unlikely there would still be griffins living there if...' He paused, staring into space. 'Griffins,' he repeated.

'Yes?' I prompted.

'Griffins are as rare as unicorns, no?'

'At least.'

'They don't live just anywhere, do they?'

'No. I mean, it's the size of them as much as anything. They need a lot of food, and a strong magickal source, especially if they're raising young.'

'Indeed,' said Alban. 'So. Where else are there known to be griffins?'

I turned back to the librarian, but Jay was way ahead of me, already asking her for every available resource on griffins.

'And Magickal Dells,' I added. 'Especially the more powerful or unusual ones.'

I could see our credit as scholars was rising by the minute with the librarian. 'Oh, we'd have lots about that,' she enthused, and off she went.

Over the next couple of hours, our scholarly spelunkings uncovered the following nuggets of information:

1: While the Court of Farringale survived on the fifth Britain, it was not home to a colony of griffins, as ours was.

2: Griffin sightings were almost as rare on the fifth as they were in our home Britain, the sixth. But, this was not because they were rare in number. It was thought to be due to their intensely magickal nature; like unicorns, they are steeped in the stuff up to their eyeballs from birth (I paraphrase here). Not only can they bear a much closer proximity to dangerously powerful magickal energies than the rest of us, they actually thrive upon it. They need it. Ergo, griffins and unicorns both tend to populate areas in which mere humans, trolls or (arguably) lesser fae fear to tread.

3: Griffins are among the most dangerous of magickal creatures, and nobody wants to tangle with them. Whole villages have been evacuated overnight when a nesting pair of griffins made themselves at home there. But, there have also been recorded cases of griffins and other races living comfortably together without incident.

4: Related to the last point, it has sometimes been known to happen that a known magickal reservoir (a poor term, for it wrongly implies that pools of magick just lie soggily about the place, begging to be dived into, which is not at all the case; but it's the best we have got) can undergo major, and apparently spontaneous, changes. Once in a great while, a Magickal Dell simply... dies, because its reservoirs dry up. On other occasions, the opposite can happen: a nice, mild Dell with just the right flows of magick can flare up without warning, flashing from balmy to deadly in a matter of hours. If we're going to go with water analogies, it would be like the placid pond at the bottom of your garden turning into a small sea. Or perhaps a wide ocean. You may not love it if this happened, but creatures like griffins would.

5: This stuff is rare. Incredibly rare. *But it happens.*

'What if it wasn't really the ortherex that destroyed Farringale?' Jay said at last. 'What if they were flooded with magick?'

Alban nodded. 'Which attracted griffins and ortherex alike, and drove away whoever was left alive after that.'

'In which case,' I said, 'perhaps Their Majesties were essentially correct after all. This *is* a natural disaster. Or on the other hand: why do Dells sometimes flood? Just because no one has yet uncovered a root cause, does not necessarily mean it's random. There haven't been enough recorded instances of it to detect patterns, or form workable theories.'

We were gathered around a circular table in one corner of the library, ignoring a growing hunger and thirst (speaking for myself, at least) in the pursuit of Knowledge. Ms.

Goodfellow had given up on us and conked out on the table top; Jay had propped a book open against her furry back. She was too deeply asleep to notice.

'Are you still working on that conspiracy theory?' Alban said to me, with a faint smile.

'That somebody deliberately destroyed Farringale? Hmm. Well. I wouldn't call it a theory, but it is a possibility that ought to be considered.'

Alban nodded. 'When we get back to Court, I'll see what the libraries have got about the last days of Farringale. Though I warn you not to get your hopes up too much. There really isn't a lot.'

'Which I can't help thinking is significant. So important and catastrophic an event ought to have more records associated with it. It ought to have been exhaustively studied.'

'Oh, it has been studied to death. There are endless pamphlets, dissertations and treatises waxing lyrical on a thousand possible causes for its demise. But since none of those authors had the benefit of actual access to the city itself, and because there's so little hard evidence to base those theories on, it's all just hot air. I suspect it's become something of a sport by now. Who can come up with the wildest theory yet?'

'Either way, Mel is right,' I said. 'If we're correct in thinking that it's a magickal surge that brought the ortherex, and the griffins, to Farringale — and keeps them there — then that's what would have to be reversed in order to restore it to safety.'

'Tall order,' said Jay.

'Truth. *Has* such a thing ever been done? Has anyone even tried?' Our stack of books, informative as they were, had given no such indication. The few recorded occasions of magickal surges, or floods, had typically devastated a village here and there, or a small town; the inhabitants had simply moved to a new, safer spot, and gone on with their lives. Nobody had considered it worth the effort of trying to retrieve a flooded site, which told me one thing at least: there was certainly no easy way to do it.

But, we had the entire Court of Mandridore on our side.

'We'll have to be the first,' said Jay.

'I feel like a hero already.'

'The ortherex and the griffins are an obstacle,' Alban pointed out.

'Right. Their Majesties will be needing significant non-troll assistance.' I beamed at him.

'Plus a couple of excellent griffin-tamers.'

'A dime a dozen, those,' I said stoutly.

'Ves. That's a lie.'

'No. It's optimism.'

Alban folded his arms. 'Same thing.'

I winced. 'Your cynicism is showing, your highness.'

I was rewarded with a scowl, which I felt was not unde-
served.

'I WANT,' I SAID shortly afterwards, as we left the library
of Whitmore and wended our way back up to Mel's spire,
'to go over the water, and see the rest of this Britain.'

'All of it?' said Jay.

'Yes.'

'That will take a while.'

'Yes.'

'Okay, I'm in.' He held up his closed fist, which I
bumped with my own.

'One crazy mission at a time?' Alban said. 'Can we do
that?'

'Fine, fine. Farringale first, *then* the world.'

Jay was clutching our stack of books, with the same ten-
derness he might show to a puppy, or his firstborn child.
He'd cared for his haul from Farringale with similar devotion. I did so like that about him. He had also undertaken
to persuade the librarian to let us abscond with them,
which had been no easy task. Even bandying Melmidoc's
name about hadn't convinced her. I wasn't sure how he

had, in the end, except that it might have had something to do with that ineffable charm of his. Put anyone in a room with Jay for long enough, and they'd do anything for him.

I probably needed to work on improving my defences.

Anyway, we'd soothed the anxious librarian with promises of leaving the books at the spire, which we assuredly would, too — right after we'd given Mauf plenty of time to canoodle with them. We wanted to take their contents with us, if we couldn't take the books themselves.

At the spire, we found Mauf deep in conversation with Mel. Loudly, too; laughter drifted through the closed door as we approached, audible even over the music, followed by snatches of some debate conducted at top volume.

'When I said they'd get along splendidly, I didn't know I was speaking the literal truth,' I said as I pushed open the door, mystified.

Mauf lay sprawled in the centre of the otherwise empty hallway, his pages drifting idly back and forth. If he wasn't a book and therefore constitutionally incapable of it, I'd have said he might be drunk.

'Miss Vesper!' he carolled joyfully as I stepped inside, Ms. Goodfellow trotting at my heels. 'Pleasant greetings!'

'Thank you,' I said, conscious of a feeling of wariness. 'And what have you two been up to?'

'This fellow knows everything — *everything* — about the seventeenth principle of magickal dynamism under controlled conditions,' said Mauf.

It was a specialty of mine, in my youth, said Melmidoc modestly.

The look on Jay's face told me he had as little notion what Mauf was on about as I did.

'We've been thieving,' I said brightly, as Jay carefully set his stack of books down by Mauf. 'With permission, I swear.'

I am astonished that Pherellina was able to provide you with such a wealth of material on the ortherex.

'She wasn't. Most of this is about Magickal Dells, surges, and griffins.'

Oh?

I told Melmidoc all about our fledgling theory. To my ear at least, it sounded very thin when spoken aloud. 'I know we've only the most circumstantial evidence as yet,' I finished. 'But we'd like to investigate further.'

I have been debating within myself during your absence, Melmidoc replied. *In fact, your excellent companion and I have had some conversation together upon a topic which may be of relevance to your quest.*

'Not the seventeenth principle of magickal dynamism under controlled conditions?' I guessed.

Not that. No. This is mere rumour, a tale, one I have long dismissed as nonsense. But perhaps it is more than that.

'Stories often contain a kernel of truth,' I offered. 'Sometimes a lot more than that.'

Indeed. Well, then. Some years after my removal here with my brother, and the most dedicated of our students and colleagues, it was suggested to me that we were not the only explorers from the sixth Britain to settle in these parts.

'What!'

Yes. We, too, were interested, at least at first. But as the story unfolded, our excitement faded, for the scenario seemed to us so replete with absurdity as to be wholly uncreditable. These other refugees were trolls, supposedly, from Farringale itself. No ordinary citizens, either; they included the highest of courtiers, prominent officials and scholars — even, so it was said, the king himself.

10

'TORVASTON THE SECOND?' I gasped. 'But no, how could that be? He and Queen Hrruna founded the new court at Mandridore.'

You see the problem. Not that I was aware of this point of detail myself, for with these snatches of rumour came no report of the catastrophe at Farringale. But in my memory, Farringale was all-powerful, utterly unassailable. Why, then, should Torvaston ever leave it? And without Hrruna? It was impossible to credit such ridiculous assertions, and I ceased to listen to those who spread them. Somewhat to my regret, now.

My brain reeling, I had no immediate idea of what to say. Alban looked absolutely thunderstruck.

'But, no,' he said, faintly. 'That cannot be, Melmidoc. It cannot. It is so widely known that Torvaston and Hrruna *both* took the Court to Mandridore. If the king had vanished, that must have been known. How could it have been concealed?'

I cannot answer that any more than you can, said Melmidoc. *And perhaps I was right to dismiss these stories; perhaps they cannot, after all, be true. But I thought that you should know of them.*

'You were right,' I said. 'Thank you, Melmidoc.' My heart was fluttering with excitement at this new mystery, and I wanted to set off running at once. What if it was true? *What if?*

'Where did they go?' said Jay. 'Was it ever said? I can't suppose they went off to your other Farringale.'

No, I do not suppose it either, Melmidoc agreed. *The Court here is similar in some respects, but wildly different in many others, and would offer nothing of the comfort of familiarity a refugee might seek. Besides which, of course, Torvaston was king only in his own Britain. Another held that position here. No, I do not think it likely they went to Farringale, but where they went instead, I never did learn.*

Alban was looking wild-eyed, and I thought I could guess at some of his thoughts. If Torvaston the Second had disappeared, who had known of it? Who knew of it now? Did his current liege-lords have the smallest suspicion?

What is commonly known about the earliest days of the new Court at Mandridore? Melmidoc asked.

'Um.' Alban visibly collected himself. 'I've never studied the details, but it's known that many of the Old Court made the transfer. Not all, but both of the monarchs for certain.' He thought for a moment, then shook his head. 'It isn't my area of expertise. I'd have to research.'

I could see two choices opening before us. We could go back to Mandridore and raid the libraries there for more information about magickal surges, griffins, and now the founding of the new Court. Or we could stay on the fifth, and see if we could uncover the truth about the supposed arrival of Torvaston the Second from the sixth. The latter posed a few problems. If nobody knew where they were said to have gone, where did we start looking?

'Mel, if we wanted to dig into these rumours, where would you suggest we go?'

If my memory does not betray me, answered Melmidoc — gliding past my abbreviation of his name, this time — *I received these rumours from the lips of a travelling storyteller. In those days, they were a common sight. They wandered from town to town, telling tales in exchange for food or ale or coin. They brought gossip, too, and the news from parts far distant, though I have often suspected them of fabricating events altogether for the sake of a wage. There are not so many, now, but a handful remain. They make a virtue of the power of tales which I, I confess, do not wholly share, but since it has lead them to keep meticulous accounts of the stories, rumours and half-truths they have told down the ages, it is not without its uses.*

'So there is a repository somewhere?' I said, encouraged.

I believe there are paper records, as I believe you are thinking of, but this practice was not begun until much more recently than the period we are interested in. I do not think it would be of much assistance to you.

'That's disappointing.'

However. There is a wild tale the storytellers like to say of themselves. It is not a simple matter to take up the profession; it is accounted among the many magickal arts, and there is a long process of learning and practice involved. When a new storyteller completes this process and takes on the mantle of tale-bearer, it is said that they receive full knowledge of all the tales that have gone before.

Melmidoc's tone became more and more sceptical as he spoke.

'You mean like a shared memory?' Jay said.

Something of that sort. I have never felt sufficient interest to enquire into the precise workings of this supposed art. I admit to finding it improbably far-fetched. But stranger things have happened.

It was impossible to argue with such a point, standing as I was in an alternate world, chatting with the ghost of a Waymaster who had died hundreds of years before. 'Where might we find one of these tale-bearers?' I asked.

There are none on Whitmore at present. However, it is common for one or more to attend the Feast of Delunia here. We may yet play host to some representative of their people.

'We can't go home yet anyway,' said Jay. 'Millie won't be ready to travel until tomorrow at the earliest.'

I chafed at the delay, wanting to talk to one of these wonderful people *now*, right away. 'Is there not some way we could track one of them down?' I asked, with faint hope.

I cannot see how. Melmidoc's voice registered suppressed amusement. *The problem with wanderers is their tendency to wander.*

'Well, then,' said Alban, with his first real smile at me all day, 'maybe it's time for that little bit of feasting we were talking about.'

'A little bit, maybe even a lot?' I said.

'Stranger things have happened.'

I will gloss over the events of that evening. Picture everything you like in the way of feasting and dancing, singing (yes, I admit it) and general decadence, and you'd have a fair idea of how Jay, Alban and I spent those hours. I'm not sorry either. Life's for living.

We retired to Millie's welcoming embrace at a shockingly late hour, only belatedly discovering that she had nothing resembling a bed among her scattered furniture. Not even one. So we divested her various chairs, couches and floors of assorted pillows, blankets and rugs, and passed out all over the floor.

It wasn't our most dignified episode.

I woke the next morning to just a touch of a headache, and an appalling crick in my neck. 'We should get Millie a few furniture upgrades,' I said to Jay, who remained too comatose to make me any response.

I found Alban nursing his own headache on the porch, which was brave of him. The sun was pretty blinding by then. 'I needed some air,' he said to me as I joined him.

'There's air inside.'

'A bit.'

You would think my stomach could've refrained from manifesting hunger, considering how much I had put into it the night before. It would have been the polite thing to do. But no. In fact it was roaring with distress.

'There's some kind of a pub two streets over,' said Alban, grinning at me.

'Pubs don't serve breakfast.'

'It's nearer lunch by now.'

I'd switched my phone off, considering it was about as useful as a lump of rock out here. I had no idea what time it was. But considering the heat of the day, the height of the sun and the stroppiness of my empty stomach, he was probably right. 'I'll fetch Jay,' I said, getting to my feet with a wince. 'If I can.'

'Bucket of cold water.'

'We have no water.'

'Ask Millie.'

'Good idea.'

Millie had no water either, but she managed a creditable alternative. Her rickety old spinet sidled over to where Jay lay prone, and struck up a thundering concerto. Millie sang along with it, with a presumably improvised song about sleeping beauty. It wasn't half bad.

Jay was insufficiently appreciative. He woke with a start, squinted blearily at the spinet's keys as they riotously played themselves, and lunged for it with a groan. 'Stop,' he begged, laying his arms over the keys to hold them down. 'Please, stop.'

Millie was undeterred.

'I do believe you've killed him,' I said, as Jay sank to the floor with a groan and, to all appearances, died.

Millie stopped at once. *Mr. Patel?*

No response.

I kicked him.

'I'm alive,' he said weakly. 'No thanks to you.'

'How does breakfast sound?'

'Terrible.'

'Coffee?'

His eyes opened. 'You could interest me in that.'

I held out a hand to him. 'Up you get. We're leaving in three minutes.'

'Only three?' Jay grasped my hand and allowed himself to be hauled to his feet, very much at my expense. I definitely don't have the kind of heft necessary for dragging grown men about.

'Four would be more than my delicate constitution could bear.' I patted my stomach.

'Ha.' Vertical again, Jay swayed unpromisingly, but managed not to collapse. 'You're about as delicate as a steel girder.'

'Is that a compliment?'

'I don't know.'

'Is it an insult?'

Jay thought about it. 'Nope.'

'Then I'll take it.'

AN HOUR AND A solid sandwich later — not to mention three cups of tea — I was feeling rather better. Even Jay looked more alive than dead after he'd imbibed a vat or two of coffee. Alban, I concluded, was some kind of demigod, and as such wholly impervious to the effects of alcohol. Or maybe he was just big.

It was as we were preparing to leave that a commotion erupted in the street outside. The music had not begun again yet, to my relief, for I was not yet up to a renewed onslaught of bone-creaking beat. But into the general quiet came the sound of distant drums beating, rapidly coming closer. The rhythm caught my attention and held it; the sounds carried the promise of excitement with them, of colour and entertainment and nameless, but desirable things, and I was seized by an urge to run after whoever was playing those drums.

I recognised a wisp or two of magick at work in all this.

Out we trooped onto the street. We were not the only ones thus affected by the music; the wide road was rapidly filling with people streaming towards the drum beats, all palpably excited about something.

I thought I heard the word "tale-bearer" as a knot of children ran breathlessly past.

'Seems promising,' I said, and trotted towards the music.

The drummer was a giant, stomping up the road with thundering footsteps, a gigantic drum slung around his neck. He beat upon the skins with his enormous fists, and the sounds echoed off the stones of the street, improbably amplified. I liked the look of him. He wore a long, sweeping coat in my very favourite colour (purple), a wide-brimmed hat over his thatch of straw-coloured hair, and his weathered face was wreathed in smiles.

Next to him trotted a woman as tiny as the drummer was tall. She was fae, perhaps from one of the sylph tribes, considering the way her feet barely seemed to touch the ground. Pale and ethereal, with a wreath of lavender hair like smoke drifting around her tiny face, she practically oozed magick as she drifted up the street towards us.

I spotted a pack train: two stout ponies laden with bulging saddle-bags.

'These look like travellers, wouldn't you say?' I observed to Jay.

'Travellers and entertainers,' he agreed.

'Let's go meet them.'

11

How it seems to work with storytellers is: they arrive, noisily. People among the quickly-gathering crowd begin shouting out requests for stories. The tale-bearers pick whichever suggestion best suits their fancy and, for a little while, the drums stop in favour of their voices. Jay, Alban and I watched for a little while, taking their measure, and heard a spirited tale of an ancient hero called Gostingot who stormed the strongholds of corrupt sorcerers an unspecified number of centuries ago. The storytellers were good: he with his great, rumbling, booming voice and she with her light, musical tones, they had everything.

Once Gostingot's tale was done, the giant resumed his drumming and off they went again, collecting more of an audience, until somebody's called-out suggestion caught their attention once more.

'This is going to take way too long,' I said, sotto voce.

'Right,' said Jay. 'It'll have to be kidnapping, then.'

I stared. 'What?'

'That is what you were going to suggest, isn't it?'

'Nothing *quite* so daring—'

'You disappoint me. Crazy Ves is becoming positively staid.'

I punched him. But only a little bit, on the arm.

I was actually looking at Alban.

'What?' said his highness, eyeing me back warily. 'I don't like that look in your eye, Ves.'

'We want tales of displaced royalty, don't we? How lucky that we happen to have a displaced royal right in our very midst. And from the same source, too!' I gave him an encouraging smile.

He sighed. 'So I am to be sacrificed for the sake of today's mission, am I?'

'Only your dignity.'

'That's reassuring.'

A short while later, a twitch or two of my intensely magickal Sunstone Wand had pepped up the prince's appearance. His simple, stylish attire now resembled something far grander: he had velvets and silks, a fine, billowing cape, and a golden coronet.

'Lose the crown, Ves,' said Alban from between gritted teeth.

'It is a bit too much,' Jay agreed, surveying the prince critically.

I pouted a bit, for it made a splendid addition to his bronze-blond locks, but I obeyed.

'And I'm not sure about the cape,' Alban added, twisting around to look at the length of it swirling behind himself. 'Must it billow like that?'

I'd given him the magickal equivalent of a wind machine. 'Of course it must. We want pomp, we want majesty, we want hints of unearthly powers from afar. We need these people to take you seriously.'

'That last part is sort of what I was getting at with the billowing thing.'

'If this were a film, you'd have all that *plus* a mantle of palpable power, crackling around your muscled frame like a lightning storm—'

'Please don't give yourself ideas, Ves.' He rolled his shoulders, stood a bit straighter, and sighed. 'Just don't let anybody trip on it, all right?'

'Will watch like a hawk,' I promised, probably mendaciously. I was given an immediate opportunity to prove myself, however, for Ms. Goodfellow made a sudden lunge at the cape's floating ends and closed her teeth around the half-corporeal fabric. I bonked her on the nose with the Wand and she sneezed in surprise, releasing the cape at once.

'You're up,' I told Alban, and nodded in the direction of the storytellers. We had ducked into a side street as they had paused again for another tale, and by the looks of it the story was winding down.

Alban closed his eyes briefly, opened them again for the pleasure of staring daggers at me, and then walked off.

'He's had practice at this,' I murmured to Jay. We watched in momentary silence as our princely prince strode, with undeniable majesty and enviable grace, across the street and approached the storytellers' audience. Somehow, that crowd parted for him like the sea; he did not even have to slow down. When he stopped, he was mere feet away from the giant and the sylph, and he seemed to my unbelieving eye to have grown a foot taller since he'd left us. Even the giant could not make him look small.

Jay and I hastily scuttled after.

'I, Prince Alban of Mandridore,' he was saying, 'have come in search of answers to an age-old mystery. My noblest of ancestors, Torvaston the Second, is said once to have visited these shores. I would know the truth of these rumours.' The fact that Alban was adopted and therefore no relation to Torvaston was quite by the by; I approved of his creative reinterpretation of the truth. He had a flare for it.

There followed some due flattering of the tale-bearers and their superior knowledge, wisdom, etc, most of which seemed to hit the mark. When he'd finished speaking, silence fell.

I noticed the giant's merry eyes had travelled from Alban to Jay to me, and there was a twinkle of amusement discernible there.

'I am sorry to tell your highness,' he said in his deep, deep voice, 'we know no tales of a Torvaston the Second.'

Alban appeared thrown by this, for when he opened his mouth nothing came out.

'However,' the giant went on, his smile broadening, 'we do mayhap know a tale of another king of the trolls, who named himself Furgidan the Dispossessed.'

I knew the word *furgidan*. It meant "king" in Court Algatish, the language spoken upon more formal occasions at the Troll Courts. The Dispossessed King. That sounded about right.

'A tale of tragedy, mystery, and adventure!' the giant went on, addressing the crowd now. 'And it takes place right here, upon your own Whitmore! Who shall hear it?'

Happily for us, the cheering that followed said *everyone* quite effectively.

'Well, then,' said the giant. 'Some hundreds of years ago, the said Furgidan arrived with a royal entourage of more than thirty trolls, all members of his former court. Dukes and barons and marchionesses all, they caused quite the stir, for they were clad in finery rather like their descendent here,' (Alban's cape billowed obligingly at these words), 'and they made the grandest of claims! "I am a king from afar," said Furgidan, "from Farringale, on another shore."

The sylph took up the tale. 'I do not know that everyone believed him, for all knew of Farringale. The splendid Court of the Trolls, rich and age-old; there could be no other. But something about these grand strangers caught at the eye, and at the heart. They had travelled long and far, for there was a weariness about them, and a melancholy.

'Offered bread and wine, the king declined, and so did all his party. They needed no sustenance, they said, and asked nothing of those who greeted them, save for one thing only. "We come in search of a home," said Furgidan. "Some distant place, rich in magick, where we will be of trouble to no one."'

'It is not known whither the dispossessed king went,' said the giant, beginning to play the soft rhythm on his drums that indicated the story was drawing to a close. 'Some say that he went into the south, to the Seas of Segorne and the islands there. Others trace his path deep into the North, to the Hyndorin Mountains and their Vales of Wonder. None can say for certain.

'But a whisper once reached my ears about Furgidan the Dispossessed. It's said that, wherever he and his courtiers made their home, they are there still. Not even the passage of centuries can defeat the lost King of Farringale.'

The tale ended there, for the giant returned to his drumming as his partner called for more requests. To my puzzlement, the drummer winked at me.

I mulled over the possible meanings of this gesture. I supposed he meant to indicate that he'd taken some liberties with the tale, which of course I had guessed. For one thing, this event — if it had taken place at all — had not happened on Whitmore, or Melmidoc would have met Furgidan the Dispossessed. Instead, only a whisper of the story had reached the Redclover brothers' ears, which argued for a much more distant setting.

For another thing, I highly doubted that Furgidan — or rather, Torvaston — and his court were still alive somewhere, three and a half centuries later. That smacked to me of a cute way of ending a tale which, in its natural form, had no real ending at all. A twist of the storytellers' art: a tendency to adapt the details of a story to suit the tastes of their audience.

And I didn't want to get started on the question of how Torvaston had known of the sixth Britain when, according to Alban, his descendants knew of only three Britains, not including this one.

But what truths might we glean from the tale, having stripped away the embellishments? Some parts of it did not altogether make sense. Then again, some parts of it were highly interesting.

We went back to the library.

'Points of interest,' I said a little later, as I stalked shelves overflowing with history books. 'Why were they weary? They had travelled far, yes, in the technical sense, but they hadn't travelled long. They must have arrived by Waymaster; they hadn't journeyed for months on foot. What was the matter with them?'

'And why were they melancholy?' Jay put in. 'Yes, they'd lost Farringale, and perhaps that's reason enough. But no mention of that was made in the story. Why did they come here, instead of going to Mandridore with the rest?'

'Third point,' said Alban, dropping a heavy tome down onto the nearest study table with a *boompf*. 'These Seas of Segorne and mountainous Vales of Wonder. Were they pulled out of thin air for the tale, because they sound good? Or were they significant? I think the latter. Look.' He riffled quickly through the book, careless of its aging paper, and skimmed a page or two. 'The Seas of Segorne,' he said. 'Place of myth, said to have existed somewhere off the southwest coast of Britain. The islands there weren't the traditional kind, for instead of floating on the water they drifted in the air, several feet above the sea's surface. It was thought that the area was so soaked in magick that it had been warped by it, and nothing there was as it should've been.'

He turned several more pages. 'Then the Hyndorin Mountains and those Wonder Vales. Same thing. Sounds to me like there were some magickal Dells scattered about up there, but unusually potent ones, flooded with magick. They, too, had gone a little strange. One was the site of a plethora of magick-induced mutations; nothing living that went in ever came out quite the same. One was said to have made a bubble of itself and floated away. Etc.' He looked at me. 'They asked for a place *rich in magick*, according to the story.'

'Not just rich, but drowning in it,' I mused. 'Even to the point of being highly unsafe.'

'Mm. But what does that do to our theory about old Farringale? If there was some kind of magickal disaster there, and the place was flooded, then it's natural that Torvaston and company would flee from it, like everyone else. But why would they go searching for another home much the same?'

'I wonder if they left voluntarily,' said Jay, leafing through a book.

'As much so as the rest, I suppose?' I said. 'Nobody wanted to abandon Farringale.'

'I don't mean Farringale, I mean Mandridore. We've been assuming that they chose to come here instead. What if they were exiled?'

'Torvaston the Second, exiled from his own court?' Alban was incredulous. 'And exiled by, presumably, his own wife? How could that be?'

'I don't know, but it would explain the melancholy, wouldn't it?'

'That might just have been a detail for the story,' Alban objected. 'Included to get the audience to pity the dispossessed king.'

'Might be,' Jay agreed. 'Then again, might not.'

I mulled this over. 'It would take something very, very big to get the king kicked out.'

'To say the least,' said Jay.

'As in, catastrophically big.' I didn't want to air the direction my thoughts were tending in. My vague new hypothesis bordered too much on the treasonous.

So I kept it to myself.

'If something like that happened,' said Alban, 'there must be some record of it at Mandridore. There must.'

'If so, I'm guessing it's deeply buried,' I said.

'Luckily, I happen to know the queen.' Alban grinned, a shade rueful.

12

I couldn't leave Whitmore again without checking on Zareen. So while Jay went off to coax Millie into an imminent departure and the baro— prince — went to consult with Melmidoc, I made my way down onto the wide beach beneath the Whitmore cliff where Ashdown Castle had settled itself. The poor old place looked the worse for wear. It was too ancient, too delicate and too run-down to be dragged the length and breadth of Britain and beyond; a part of its roof had caved in during the journey (to Val's cost), and, robbed of the foundations it was used to, it had... shifted, in places. The effect was a general sagging, as of a crestfallen building enjoying a lengthy sulk.

I felt rather sorry for it. You'd think Fenella would be more careful with her family's ancestral home.

Inside, the air was much colder than the sun-drenched outdoors. That's the way with old buildings: all that brick and stone and none of the insulation, double-glazing and so on that characterises more modern structures. But there was something unearthly about the chill in the great, shadowy hall, and I moved with caution. Last time I had set foot in there, the walls had been weeping great, salt tears. The ten or so enslaved Waymasters who'd moved the place had not been at all happy about it.

Was Zareen even still there? I wandered down a corridor or two, feeling like the only moving object for about twelve miles. The castle had the hushed, too-still air of total desertion. 'Zar?' I called, though not very loudly. I had the irrational feeling that a loud noise might bring the rest of the roof down.

Miranda popped into my thoughts. I'd last seen her somewhere in these castle halls, too. She couldn't still be here — surely she had been dispatched back to our own Britain with the rest of her new colleagues. But when I came to consider the idea, I found I was not entirely sure. Distracted, exhausted and confused, I hadn't thought to make certain that she was among the throng we had crammed into Millie's parlours a few days before. 'Mir?' I called.

No response. My footsteps made discouraging dull, ringing sounds on the tiled floors, and the echoes they sent up told me clearly enough that I was alone.

Which is why I nearly died of fright when a voice abruptly screamed: '*Is someone there?*'

'Argh!' I said, and fell against the nearest wall. I regretted this at once, for it oozed a freezing chill which went straight to my bones. I hurriedly leapt away again. 'Er. It's only me,' I said, squinting into the pervasive gloom. I saw no one. 'Ves of the Society. No threat to you whatsoever.'

'You should not be here,' said the voice. 'The ghost witch promised no one would come in.'

Ghost witch? 'You mean Zareen?'

'Yes.'

'I came to visit the ghost witch. I'm a friend. Do you know where she is?'

'She is engaged at present and cannot receive visitors.'

'You mean she isn't here?'

'Oh, she is,' said the disembodied voice, a note of disgust creeping in. 'She is busy. With the *man.*'

I was not altogether surprised to hear that George Mercer was not making himself popular. 'Can you tell me where she is?' I persevered.

'Northwest tower,' the voice snapped.

'Ah. And where is—'

'Up the stairs.'

My enquiries for more specific directions went unanswered, so with a sigh I toiled up the first flight of stairs I came to, their simple design and shabby state informing me that I had wandered into the servants' quarters. I toddled down passages uncounted, through drawing-rooms and bedchambers and parlours, aided only by an occasional snappish interjection from my bad-tempered guide: '*Not* that way. *The other door!*' At length, a promisingly spiralling stairwell together with the low murmur of voices (hopefully the living variety) told me I had come to the right place.

Pausing near the top of the stairs, I called: 'Zar?'

The murmuring stopped.

'I hope you're Ves,' came Zareen's voice.

'What if I'm not?'

'George will blast you out of existence.'

'I don't see why I have to be obliterated by George, of all people. That's just adding insult to injury. Can't you do it?'

The rickety oak door creaked open, and Zareen appeared. She was not wearing a great deal.

Neither, I soon had occasion to note, was George.

I gave a cough. 'Everything's going well then, hm?'

'Some things,' Zareen corrected. 'Some things are going well.'

George, lounging in a threadbare chair near the window, scowled at me, a greeting I returned with similarly warm feelings. I'd learned enough about Zareen's past to excuse her lingering infatuation with George — if that's what it was — but that didn't mean I had to like the man myself.

'What are you doing back here?' Zareen said. 'I didn't think we'd be seeing you for a while.'

'On a royal mission.' I grinned.

'Troll Court?'

'How'd you know?'

'Wild guess: has to be something to do with that smooth talker of a baron.'

I toyed with the idea of enlightening Zareen on the point of the smooth-talker's identity (and marital status), but decided against it. Not with George hanging around. We could have that conversation later.

I also couldn't tell her much about the mission, though her lack of questions suggested she knew that. 'Do you two need anything?' I asked instead.

'Nope, we're good.'

'Righto. And how's Operation Ashdown progressing? I gather George is killing it with the locals.'

'So you met Harriet.'

'If she's the snappish lady with the man-hating attitude, then yes.'

Zareen grinned at George, who rolled his eyes. 'Harriet Theale, vicar's wife. She has ideas about propriety. I'm afraid our modern attitudes aren't working for her at all.'

'How sisterly of her to blame George instead of you.'

'It's only fair. Normally the girls get all the blame. Ves, I should tell you: we're not bringing Ashdown home.'

Unexpected. 'What?' I said, my brows going up.

'You've seen the state of it, no? I don't believe it can bear another cross-world hop. Nor should it be expected to. We're looking instead for a better, permanent home for it out here on the fifth. Obviously it can't stay on the beach.'

'You don't think Fenella will want it back?'

'I dare say she will, but that's tough. She shouldn't have used it like a bus service in the first place. Once the Waymasters here have had time to recover, we'll coach them through one final removal, get the castle set down somewhere more stable, and then let them go.'

'They won't want to go back to their own Britain?'

'You're full of discouraging questions, Ves.'

'Sorry.'

Zareen shrugged. 'That's a bridge we'll cross when we get there. Any that want to go home... well, I'm hoping Melmidoc might be able to help, either way.'

He might, at that. Perhaps he could get some of them settled in their own houses. After all, Whitmore seemed to make rather a habit of it.

George was, as usual, silent. Was it just that he hated me, or was he taciturn by nature? Presumably he was more forthcoming with Zareen. 'Thank you for sticking with Zar,' I said to him. 'She's important to us.'

'And to me.' Three ungracious words.

I gave up.

'Right, leaving,' I said. 'One thing, though. Have you seen Miranda about?'

'Didn't she get shipped back to the sixth with the rest?'

'I think so, and at the same time I don't think so.'

'We haven't seen her.'

'Roger.' Perhaps it was thinking of Miranda that led to my saluting Zareen. 'Vesper out. Take care out here, hm?'

'We're okay. You go impress the socks off the troll king.'

'Actually, I get the impression the queen rules the roost there.'

'As it should be.'

I arrived at Millie's farmhouse to find Alban and Jay both there before me. Millie's front door hung open; I sauntered in. A delicate melody wafted through the rooms, emanating, I supposed, from Millie's old spinet. But it was not Millie playing it; it was Jay.

I regarded him in silence for a moment, enjoying the sheer beauty of the music he played. I'd rarely heard any- thing like it before. Indeed, had I ever? The music floated and danced, like... like faerie bells, I wanted to say, though stifled the thought as too fanciful by half.

'Did I know you could play?' I said, when Jay's fingers stilled upon the keys.

He jumped, and gave me a startled glance over his shoulder. 'Hi Ves.'

'That was beautiful.'

He didn't answer, but he did smile. 'Alban's upstairs,' he said. 'Are you ready to go?'

'Yes. What's he doing upstairs?'

'Hiding from me.'

'Uh huh. And why does he need to hide from you?'

'We might have had words.'

'I hope it was nothing to do with me.'

Jay's silence spoke volumes.

All right, so Jay was still angry with Alban for flirting with me when he shouldn't have. Why? Did I seem broken-hearted? I didn't think I was. Absolutely not. Not even disappointed, really. Not a bit.

I went upstairs.

Alban sat tucked into the embrace of a pretty window seat in the homely drawing-room, one of its few pretences at elegance. He was too big for it, but had curled himself into it anyway with splendid disregard for proportion. Staring, no doubt moodily, out of the window, he did not turn when I came in.

I was swiftly growing tired of talking to people's backs. 'What did Melmidoc have to say about our theory?' I asked without preamble.

'He thinks it insane.'

'Excellent.'

'He might be right. No Court would exile its own king, and no exiled king would go in search of precisely the same dangerous environment he had just fled from. But then, Melmidoc does have a grudge or two against the Troll Court. His opinion is hardly clear-sighted.'

'I say we proceed.'

'Seconded. I can't think of a better idea.'

'Does he know of a way to, uh, drain magick from a flooded Dell?'

'No. Says it's never been done anywhere, to his knowledge.'

'I suppose no one's had reason enough to brave the dangers.'

He nodded without answering, and finally looked at me. It seemed to cost him an effort. 'He's right, of course.'

'Melmidoc?'

'Jay. I've been a selfish dick.'

'Were those Jay's words?'

'I paraphrase.'

I felt the beginnings of a headache coming on. 'Jay has no right to attack you for it,' I said briskly. 'I believe I can understand the difficulties of your predicament. And I don't need to be protected from you or anybody else.'

'So you aren't hurt?'

'No.' I said it stoutly, without a trace of doubt, and met Alban's eyes squarely when he looked at me.

He held my gaze for a moment, then nodded and looked away. 'That is good to know.'

His tone suggested he'd drawn all manner of conclusions from that single word, some of which may or may not be hurtful, and some of which may or may not be true. But I didn't have time to deal with it just then. Trailing from Zareen and George in dishabille, to an indignant Jay, to a sulking Alban, I felt like a nanny with a large and fractious brood to manage. 'We'd better go, hadn't we?'

It is awfully romantic, Millie broke in. *Like a fairy tale. Shall you marry the prince in the end, Miss Vesper? I do hope so!*

If I'd tried to come up with the quickest way to make the scene even more painfully awkward, I couldn't have done a better job. 'Thanks, Millie,' I said with a sigh.

I judged it best to beat a hasty retreat.

I like her, I heard Millie say before I had made it out of earshot.

And Alban said, softly, 'Me too.'

13

The library of Mandridore is to die for.

I mean that almost literally. I'm sure I felt my heart stop when we walked in.

Tall people need a tall library, yes? This one soared up and up and *up*, to such a height there were wisps of cloud drifting near the ceiling. If there was a ceiling. No word of a lie, there really were, though I don't suppose they ever took it upon themselves to rain. Every inch of every wall was covered in shelves housing perfectly-ordered rows of books. I looked for the traditional long ladders winding up the bookcases, but of these there was no sign. I did, however, spot a large tome floating at a leisurely pace down from a distant shelf. At Mandridore, one did not travel to the books; the books travelled to you.

I could get used to such a place.

'When I die,' I heard Mauf say from inside my satchel, 'bury me here.'

I hoped he was busy soaking up whatever he could get his filthy book-mitts upon.

A dash of magick kept the light levels on the muted side, the better to protect the collections. This lent the library's several chambers a peaceful, serene air which could not but please. I'd walked in and felt immediately at ease.

Unfortunately, things did not go nearly so well as this auspicious beginning suggested.

While Jay wandered off to browse, drawn like a magnet to a floor-level shelf crowded with enormous leather-bound volumes, I went with Alban to the grand mahogany desk behind which sat the librarian on duty. A large, handsome woman of middle age, she became flustered at Alban's approach, and dropped a brief curtsey. Some subtle change to Alban's expression told me he did not welcome this deference.

'Dame Hellenna, I wonder if you could help us,' he said, with an approximation of his usual smile. 'We are interested in anything you can find on the topic of Torvaston the Second. Periods of particular interest include directly before, and any time after, the fall of Farringale.'

I did not at all see why, but something about this request made Dame Hellenna nervous. She glanced uncertainly at me, then made for the bookshelves with the air of a woman running away.

A slight frown creased Alban's brow.

The jumpy librarian soon returned. 'I— I'm afraid there are no books available on those topics, sir,' she said, not meeting his eye.

'None?' repeated Alban blankly.

Dame Hellenna shook her head.

'How can that be? King Torvaston founded this Court!'

The librarian began to look most unhappy. 'I quite see your point, sir, but nonetheless...'

'You're telling me,' said Alban with forced calm, 'that no one has written of Mandridore's founders in nearly four centuries?'

'If they have, sir, their books are not kept here.'

'That is impossible. There must be something.'

I laid a hand on Alban's arm, for he seemed to be working himself into a froth. 'Forgive me,' I said to Dame Hellenna, 'but *were* there any books on those topics, at any time in the past?'

Her eyes got a bit shifty. 'I... couldn't say, madam.'

Uh huh.

Alban was all over that like a rash. 'So there aren't now but that hasn't always been the case. When were they removed, and by whose order?'

'They— I don't— I don't precisely know, sir, but...' She glanced about, as though she might be overheard, though no one was nearby save for myself. 'I know of no specific removal of those books, but there are records of a general purge undertaken some years ago, by order of your highness's mother's esteemed father.'

It took me a moment to parse that. The queen's dad, or Alban's adoptive grandfather. Got it.

'The library *was* overfull, of course, though so it always is...'

'How many books were taken out?' said Alban crisply.

'The records suggest a great many, sir, though few titles are listed by name.'

'When was this?'

'More than fifty years ago.'

Well, well. Interesting. A spot of spring-cleaning would make a good cover for the removal of a few inconvenient books, though I failed to see why a former royal would have wanted to. What had he found out about Torvaston?

Did Alban's mother know?

I could see similar questions echoing through Alban's thoughts, for he'd developed a grim demeanour, and a note of worry lurked in his eyes.

Dame Hellenna appeared to be suffering some second thoughts. 'I... beg your highness will not inform the queen of my comments, sir. My job—'

'I need not mention your name,' Alban said, in a fractionally softened tone. 'Thank you for your help, Hellenna.'

Upon which words we turned away, leaving poor Dame Hellenna to recover her poise.

Jay was happily installed at a table with a stack of no fewer than eight gigantic tomes beside him. They were too big for the table, so he'd piled them up on the floor beside him. The heap was half as tall as I was.

'I'm sorry to interrupt your book party,' I said, with more sincerity than probably appeared, for he *did* look happy. 'We have hit a snag.' I told him about the Torvaston problem.

Jay regarded Alban thoughtfully. 'So his highness is off to lay the smack down on her majesty?'

'Something like that.'

'While he's doing that.' Jay turned a page the size of a small sail, and the word *Farringale* caught my eye. An exquisitely detailed drawing depicted a block of several rooms, gathered together like a honeycomb. After a moment, the penny dropped: Farringale's library. This must be where Alban had copied his hand-drawn map from. Jay looked up at me. 'We could trawl from library to library looking for lost books, but it seems to me there's only one place we can be sure of discovering the truth.'

'You want to go back to Farringale?'

'Don't you?'

No. Yes. I did, sort of? And at the same time I really didn't. I'd suspected, since the beginning, that our going there was precisely what Their Majesties had in mind when they'd summoned us to the Court. 'I don't want to do it alone,' I said. 'Nor can we, really, since we'll need House's help if we want the third key back.'

'Do you think Milady will agree to partnering with the Court on this? She was against our ever going there in the first place.'

'True,' I conceded. 'But since we came out alive, and with some highly interesting books in tow, I've some hopes she might have changed her mind.'

'Right. We can't take the baron this time, though.' Jay sat back in his chair, and glanced perfunctorily at Alban. 'Sorry, I mean the prince.'

Alban's brow went up.

'Too dangerous for you,' said Jay. 'We could have stayed longer the last time, if we hadn't had to evacuate you.'

'There is now a cure,' Alban pointed out, presumably referring to the condition of ortherex... infestation, or whichever charming term by which one might discuss that disease.

'Which has never been tested in Farringale,' I pointed out. 'As danger zones go, that place is code red. And you're the crown prince, for heaven's sake. I can't believe Their Majesties let you go in the first place.'

Alban busied himself adjusting the cuff of his left sleeve. I received the impression he was avoiding my eye.

'Oh,' I said. 'You didn't ask them.'

'I had their authority in the same way that you had Milady's.'

'Touché.'

'YOU FOUND *NOTHING*?' SAID Queen Ysurra perhaps half an hour later. Alban had escorted us back to Their Majesties' manor, but not to the Topaz Parlour. The queen sat, surprisingly, in the kitchen, sorting an array of dried flowers across the top of an aged, much-scrubbed oak table. There was no sign of the king.

'Not precisely nothing,' I said placatingly. I was perched atop a stool on the other side of the table, with a glass of clear, cold water before me. I was more disconcerted than encouraged by this peculiar simplicity. I'd only just begun to get used to all the pomp and gilding. 'The ortherex simply aren't such a problem in the fifth Britain. They are viewed as pests, like rats. Which means, the conditions which led to their total overrun of old Farringale may well be unique. So. If we can find out precisely what those conditions are, and how the parasites came to proliferate so excessively, then perhaps we can reverse those changes. If we can, the ortherex will die out.'

'Which they should have, already,' said Jay. 'There are no trolls left alive there, and nothing but raw magick for the creatures to eat. That makes no sense. We can't find an answer to these mysteries in another world; Melmidoc had no idea what we were talking about, and Whitmore's library had nothing. We need to go deep into Farringale itself, and take a look with our own eyes.'

Queen Ysurra carefully crumbled desiccated lavender into a bowl, wafting pungent aromas everywhere. I took a deep, grateful inhalation. I've always found it a relaxing scent, and perhaps so did Her Majesty. 'I cannot deny that I had hoped for just such a venture in time,' she said, after a moment's thought. 'But not in so ill-prepared a fashion. What do you propose to do?'

'We would like the Court to partner with the Society,' I said. 'Jay and I will spearhead this mission, but we would like our own allies with us. And we'd like to do it with your blessing, and Milady's — not least because we'll need every resource either organisation can put at our disposal.'

Queen Ysurra's gaze went to Alban.

'We won't be taking Alban with us,' I said quickly. 'Not into such danger.'

That apparently wasn't what was on her mind. 'Do you really think my father knew something about this?' she said in a low voice.

'It looks that way,' said Alban softly. 'It does seem that he was hiding something about Torvaston.'

The queen looked, suddenly, haggard, and I remembered what Alban had said about her health. She sagged over the table top, weary beyond even her advanced years.- 'We had no thought, when we began with this ill-fated idea, that there could be any scandal attached.'

I began to feel afraid that she might refuse us. 'Our promise, your majesty,' I said firmly. 'We are well used to keeping secrets. It is to be hoped we will find nothing to the detriment of your family, but if we do... provided it endangers no one, we undertake to keep it to ourselves. This I can promise on behalf of the Society as a whole.'

I suppose so conditional a promise was not as reassuring as Ysurra might have liked, but she sighed, and gave me a nod. 'I cannot prevent your going. Not when Naldran and I opened this can of worms ourselves. But I beg you to be... careful.'

A host of different warnings could be read into those words. Careful of what? Everything? Everything. It was, after all, a dangerous place. Ortherex might be dangerous mostly to trolls, but we did not absolutely *know* that they wouldn't attack us. There were griffins, too, and that was just scratching the surface. What if we were right, and it was magick-flooded? What else might we find when we lingered in those ruined halls?

My stomach fluttering with a mix of excitement and fear, I stood up and gave Her Majesty my best curtsey. 'With your leave, majesty, we'll get going immediately. No time like the present.'

Queen Ysurra just looked at me, and her face was grey. 'Thank you, Miss Vesper,' she said. 'Mr. Patel. Alban will see that you receive everything you need.'

'A couple of keys to Farringale, for a start,' I said. 'The third one's our problem.'

14

'You want to do... what?' said Milady, some twen-ty-four hours later.

'Pop back into Farringale, ascertain the true cause of its infestation and consequent demise, mend it, divest it of its juiciest books by way of our well-earned reward, and be home in time for tea,' I said smoothly.

'Is the tea strictly vital to the mission?'

'When have I ever been willing to miss tea?'

I chose to interpret Milady's subsequent silence as either amusement or a hearty endorsement of the plan, and wait-ed.

'Ves,' she said at last. 'This is ambitious, even for you.'

'What if I told you it was Jay's plan?'

'Hey,' Jay objected. 'My plan was to go into Farringale on a research and exploration mission. Scientific. Information gathering. That kind of thing.'

'Right, sorry,' I murmured. 'I might have got a little carried away with the rest.'

'If you find yourself with the means to restore the city then by all means use them,' said Milady, with just a *hint* of sarcasm. 'One suspects the situation might prove too complicated to mend by tea-time, however.'

When Milady starts referring to herself as "one", she's at maximum satire. 'All right, we'll take tea with us,' I said sunnily.

The air sparkled. Definitely laughter; hopefully the nice kind. 'May one ask what you are doing asking *my* permission?' Milady continued.

Perhaps not the nice kind.

'We'll need Rob,' I said. 'And I'd like Indira, too.'

'Wait, what?' said Jay.

'On the grounds that there's little Team Patel can't deal with,' I went on, doggedly. 'We'll need the usual toys from Stores—'

'Including that Sunstone Wand Ornelle has been complaining to me about?' said Milady drily.

Since the object in question currently lay at the bottom of my satchel, with Ms. Goodfellow asleep on top of it, I smoothly let this pass. 'And of course, we'll need House to lend us the third key again.'

'Ves,' said Milady firmly. 'Forgive me for pointing this out, but you would divest me of every single one of these advantages, without a word and without compunction, if you thought it necessary. So I ask you again: why are you asking my permission?'

'Is it too much to believe that I'd like to do things by the book this time?'

'Yes.'

Jay folded his arms and lifted his brows at me. The look said: *Well. Go on.*

So nice to have back-up.

'Sneaking takes so much time and effort,' I tried.

'Undoubtedly, but Farringale has been lost for some four centuries already. It will await your kind, liberating efforts for another day or two.'

Unanswerable.

'I miss Home,' I said. I tried to sound nonchalant but I'm afraid the words came out in rather a small voice.

'You what?' said Milady. Even Jay looked a little surprised.

'I miss Home,' I said again. 'I miss the Society. I miss my friends, and I miss you, even when you are witheringly sarcastic. I dislike being rogue and I want my family back.' I paused. No one spoke. 'Seeing as there's no way the Ministry or anyone else could reasonably object to our assisting the Troll Court with a research expedition, I see no reason to go on playing the loose cannon while we do it.'

'I see,' said Milady, in something of a softened tone.

I avoided Jay's eye while I awaited her verdict.

'The matter of the fifth Britain is not yet resolved,' she warned. 'Not to mention whatever remains of the other seven. I had hoped to use the three of you to uncover more.'

'You still can.'

'Which cannot be done under the official aegis of the Society, for the Ministry is still being woefully stubborn upon that topic.'

My heart sank a little more with every syllable, but I tried not to let it show. 'I understand,' I said, which was true, though I didn't like it.

'However,' said Milady. 'The topic of Farringale is a loaded one. Its mythological status rivals that of Atlantis in some quarters. Were it to be widely known that we are launching an exploratory expedition, I fear we would be somewhat interfered with.'

My tension eased a fraction. 'Most irritatingly,' I agreed.

'House, of course, is a related but separate entity and any choices made by her are little to do with me,' she continued.

I was intrigued by this use of *her* to refer to the House. I don't think I had ever heard Milady designate a gender before.

'I will lend you Rob and Indira for one week, together with any supplies they should find it necessary to withdraw from Stores. You may not be aware, but Their Majesties of Mandridore recently communicated to me an urgent need for expert consultants in certain fields in which Rob and Indira excel. Naturally, we at The Society are always ready to assist the Court.'

I concealed a smile. 'We'll be very discreet,' I promised. 'Maximum sneaking.'

'What's more,' said Milady, and the air glittered. 'Tea will be provided.'

'Typical Milady chicanery,' I said to Jay half an hour later, as we sat waiting in a tiny back-parlour somewhere on the ground floor at Home. 'If anyone asks inconvenient questions, she can simply blame the Court. And fairly enough. We *are* employed by them at present, after all, and they've got the might to out-manoeuvre the Ministry, if necessary.'

Jay slowly shook his head. 'I may never get used to the double-speak.'

'Give it time.'

'Does she ever say *no* and, um, mean it?'

'Frequently.'

'Right.'

Confusion radiated off poor Jay, but one couldn't explain these things.

We'd been sent down to the parlour to "wait", officially, until Rob and Indira were ready to join us. Actually, we were hiding. The Society is full of wonderful, loyal people (I see no occasion to remember Miranda at this moment), but wherever there are people there will be gossip, and we did not want the grapevine ruining all our devious plans. Let them talk, if they would — *after* we'd got the goods.

I'd delivered a wish list to Rob, who'd promised to stop by Stores on his way down. I'd chosen him rather than Indira because, as charming as Jay's sister could be (when she forgot to be shy), Rob had a way about him. I suspected Ornelle of being either a little afraid of his mildly forbidding air, or of harbouring a secret crush. The latter would hardly surprise me. Rob's a good-looking man, with or without the greying hair, and underneath the grim exterior he's marshmallow.

A few inches away from my feet, the floor bubbled. Considering that it was, in its entirety, paved with well-worn flagstones and carpeted with equally well-loved rugs, not a whole lot of bubbling should've been happening.

'I think this is our key,' I said to Jay.

We watched with spellbound fascination as a patch of stone a few inches wide buckled and boiled, belched bubbles into the air, and finally expelled a glittering key. I snatched it up. Its smooth silver, only slightly tarnished, was untouched by the churning goop, and its inset sapphire glowed.

'Thank you,' I said to House.

The floor settled back into its usual smooth, unbelching configuration.

I paused to consider. House could have simply put the key into my hand; what did the swampy-floor routine betoken? Did it — *she* — disapprove of our return into Farringale? She had helped us the last time, even without Milady's concurrence. Now, it seemed, the situation was rather the reverse; Milady had persuaded, but House was not pleased.

'Do you dislike the prospect, darling House?' I said aloud. 'Is it the possible restoration of the city that you dislike? Surely not.'

There came no reply, a silence I was unsure how to interpret.

'It will only be opened again if it is no longer dangerous,' I assured the building. 'Any such outcome is likely to be some way off, if it is ever feasible.'

Silence.

'You're worried about Ves,' said Jay suddenly. 'You think she's reckless.'

The floor belched loudly.

Did that mean Jay was right, or did it mean that House rained scorn upon the very notion that it might be concerned?

'We aren't trolls,' I put in. 'We should be safe enough from the ortherex.' Even I had to wince at the unpromising word *should* in the middle of my sentence.

'And we're pretending the griffins don't exist, just now,' Jay added helpfully.

'We survived them last time!'

'So we did.'

I glowered at Jay. 'It was your idea to go. Have you forgotten that?'

'Nope.' He smiled at me.

The floor belched out another bubble, this time rather nearer to Jay.

'Too right,' I said. 'If we're eaten by griffins, it is all Jay's fault.'

'In which case, if we save the city, that is my fault, too,' said Jay.

'Deal.'

Secretly I was proud of Jay. I was having a deliciously bad influence on him.

'ORNELLE WANTS HER WAND back,' Rob told me when he finally showed up, a full hour later.

'But it loves me.'

He grunted. 'We all do, more's the pity. Ornelle knows she stands zero chance.' He was offloading objects into my welcoming arms as he spoke: some of Orlando's sleep capsules (they're my style, all right?); a few bottomless phials filled with various restoratives; an emergency porridge-pot (I know, I know. Porridge isn't my favourite food for the road either, but one takes what one can get and a steady diet of gruel is at least *way* better than gnawing hunger); and one of those scroll-and-quill combos I may have mentioned before. Val had the other one. If our phones should fail while we were out there, I didn't want to be totally incommunicado.

Jay received a Wand of his own: the Ruby, very flashy. I gazed long upon it.

'Stop it,' said Rob. 'You've already purloined one of the best Wands we've got.'

I cast him a sheepish smile, and tried my best to put a lid on my covetousness as he handed a beautiful Wand to

Indira. It looked, to my experienced eye, like the Spinel: clear purple with a pinkish shimmer.

'Thank you both for coming along,' I said, with a smile especially for Indira. She, as always, said little, and besides offering a shy smile back, stood waiting in patient immobility. I was surprised to see that her broken arm was fully mended already. She'd been benefiting from some of Rob's more potent healing enchantments.

Rob was senior enough to have his own Wand on permanent assignment, of course. He'd been wielding the Lapis Lazuli beauty for years. He generally wore it strapped to the inside of his arm, right alongside those deadly charmed knives of his.

I did a quick supply survey. Shiny toys from Stores: check. Alban's map of Farringale City: check. Lady Tregawny's *Recollections of a Lost Age: A Courtier's Memories of Farringale,* purloined from Mandridore Library: check. Talkative, well-informed book named Mauf: check.

Jay, Rob, Indira and Ms. Goodfellow: check checkity check.

Me. Emphatic check.

'Ready for adventure, danger and glory?' I said, hefting my shoulder bag.

'Lead on,' said Rob.

'Onward,' said Jay.

Indira nodded emphatically.

'Right, then.'
Off we went.

IT FELT LIKE OLD times as we trooped down to the Waypoint in the cellar, a Society team once more. I hated a bit that I could say things like *feels like old times* about such a subject, and after only a few weeks of supposed independence, but I put that aside.

The journey proceeded much as before. Jay whisked us down to the Winchester area the quick-and-speedy way. I was pleased to note that my nausea was lessening with every Way-journey; either I was becoming a better Traveller of the Ways, or practice was improving Jay's technique as Waymaster. Either way, I arrived in a Winchester field with my dignity intact and my spirits high.

After that, it was my turn. I fished up my syrinx pipes. (Will it surprise you to learn that I wasn't really, technically, allowed to keep them? Their coming into my possession at all was more by accident than design, and there were those who'd objected strenuously to so rare and powerful a Treasure falling into such untested hands as mine were at the time. Milady made sure I got to keep them. I'm still not sure why).

Addie and Friends made excellent time, as is their wont. We swooped through the skies, wafted elegantly by unicorn wings, and landed near the bridge over the River Alre within half an hour. It was only mid-morning and the day stretched ahead of us, bright with possibility even if it *was* raining a bit.

I was soon grateful for my decision to request Indira.

'I am too short,' I said with chagrin, standing beneath the high-arching bridge with three keys in my hand and no way of reaching the trio of alcoves into which they needed to be set. Last time, we'd had Alban with us, who was plenty tall enough for the job. This time, our tall folk included only Rob and Jay, neither of whom had sufficient inches.

Indira subjected the bridge to one of her swift, keen looks, swept the keys out of my hands, and rose smoothly into the air by a distance of several feet. She levitated with the grace of a gazelle, while I (despite my aptitude with the flying chair trick) do so with all the elegance of an exuberant young bullock. What's more, she could hold herself perfectly steady, the better to manipulate the tricky keys-and-alcoves combinations. Naturally, she needed no help discerning which key went where. Within minutes she had all three inset, and red, green and blue lights blazed over the bridge.

'Right,' said Rob as a door lit up in the ageing brick, and swung slowly inward. 'Ves and me first. Shield, please, Ves. Make it a good one.'

I don't fly well, but I do Ward. I shrouded us both in a tough shield charm, tuned to repel (hopefully) just about anything we might imminently encounter: poison, fire, lightning, physical attacks, incoming curses, hexes or other magickal unpleasantries, and more. It hadn't the faintest chance of repelling a serious griffin attack, of course, but one does one's little best.

In we went.

Last time we had ventured into Farringale, we'd found an empty but eerily tidy city, marred by scattered pools of stagnant water but otherwise largely intact. It had been utterly silent, of course, that heavy silence one finds in long-abandoned spaces.

This time was different. This time, we walked into chaos.

15

'WHAT THE BLOODY HELL?' growled Rob, staring in awe.

I had no words to offer. They'd all gone.

If I'd wondered before how an abandoned city came to be so well-kept, I had my answer now. Farringale's wide, white boulevard lay stretched before us, flanked on either side by grand mansions in pale or golden stone and brick. A legion of shabby broomsticks was abroad in the street, wielded by no one and yet engaged in a furious orgy of sweeping. The noise bordered upon cacophonous as bristles scraped ruthlessly over paving stones and pathways and walls, removing every speck of accumulated dirt and dust. Ragged shreds of cloth applied themselves to leaded window panes, buffing them up to a renewed shine. Greenish water drained slowly from collected puddles, and buckets of fresher, soapy water emptied themselves into the spaces they left behind, the brooms rushing in to scrub away the stains left by filth and algae.

The air freshened slowly as we watched, the aromas of stagnation fading in favour of wafting, floral fragrances.

I kept my shield up and sturdy, in case any of the household implements should take exception to our entrance and attempt to attack us. They did not. We went ignored as they completed their furious spring-cleaning, those that approached routing smoothly around us with the apparent ease of long practice.

After, perhaps, ten minutes of this, a bell tinkled brightly somewhere and this seemed to be a signal, for the broomsticks and cloths, buckets and brushes, all vanished with a concerted *pop*.

I thought, apropos of nothing and with a brief pang, of Alban. What a pity he had missed the broomstick ballet.

'How do we get this at home?' said Jay, who had come up next to me some minutes before.

'We've a lesser version of it at Home already,' I said. 'Much lesser, and more discreet. I can't imagine the kind of power it would take to operate the Sweeping Symphony on so large a scale.'

'And who's running it, anyway?' said Rob. 'Any symphony needs a conductor.'

'Do you think someone is still alive out here?' I said, thinking of Baroness Tremayne, the... shade, I suppose, of a former courtier I'd met on our previous visit. But no, she was not technically alive. Not technically dead, either, but hers was a shadowed existence. She was, surely, too distant from the material world to much affect it. That was how she'd managed to survive at all.

'It's hard to see how,' said Rob, with which opinion I had to agree. Even if somebody non-troll had lingered in Farringale after the fall, and successfully avoided the ortherex, how could they survive so long here? Why would anyone try? There was nothing left — no food, no trade, no links with the outside world at all.

No, there had to be another explanation.

'I suppose this answers your question about the corpses of the fallen,' I said to Jay. 'They were, um, tidied away.'

'How efficient,' he answered. 'I wonder if the Symphony always had that function.'

'Or if somebody added it in later, as need arose? Perhaps.'

Indira had the strained look of a young woman trying her damnedest to commit a wealth of information to memory. She was probably brilliant enough to figure out its workings at a glance. By next week, the Sweepers at Home might be receiving a significant upgrade.

'There was a pattern to their movements,' she suddenly said. 'They weren't as random as they seemed. It was fully choreographed.'

That interested me. 'Could something so complicated survive indefinitely without direct oversight?'

'Not easily,' she said, and I caught the scholar's gleam sparking in her dark eyes. It's that rabid fervour some of us get when presented with a mystery. She *had* to find the answer. 'There would have to be a strong anchor somewhere, something with a powerful and renewing source of magick. Probably with a web of smaller anchors across the city...' her slender hands sketched a rapid grid-shape in the air, and she drifted away towards the nearest building, eyes alight.

'Indira,' I called, not without a certain reluctance. 'Now's not the time. Dangers, remember?'

Not that we had seen hide nor hair of any so far. The broomsticks were indifferent to us, and though the twilight-blue heavens roiled with snowy and golden clouds and crackled with lightning, as they had before, no griffin had swooped out of the skies to destroy us.

Nonetheless, I may be Ves but I am not *that* reckless.

'Right,' said Indira and drifted back, with only one, lingering look of regret at the pale brick structure she'd been heading for.

'I'd like to find that anchor,' said Rob.

'And whatever source it's drawing from,' added Jay.

'Seconded upon both counts,' I said. 'I'd also like to see what Goodie makes of this place.'

'Goodie?' echoed Indira.

'Goodie Goodfellow, AKA Robin, AKA Pup.' I hauled her out of the satchel as I spoke, ignoring her little grunt of protest — honestly, has there ever been a creature more addicted to slumber? — and set her down. 'Goodie,' I said in my stern voice. 'We need your help. Find interesting stuff, but — and this is important — *no running away.* Understood?'

Ms. Goodfellow's nose was already glued to the ground by the time I'd made it through half of this speech, and she took off at a rolling trundle, tail wagging. I was left to hope that the main gist of my instructions had got through to her somehow.

'Not to mention,' I said as I set off after her, 'the library. Post-haste.'

'Seconded,' said Mauf from the vicinity of my shoulder bag.

'Haven't you spent enough time on those shelves already?' This was inaccurate, of course; I sometimes forgot he was only identical to Bill the Book, not *actually* Bill. But since he was a copy, and possessed all of Bill's knowledge, it amounted to much the same thing. Right?

'I am over familiar with some portion of the library,' said Mauf, 'and I trust you will not be disposed to leave me there. But I anticipate an exploration of the rest of my colleagues with great eagerness.'

His colleagues, I supposed, were books. I anticipated the same myself, most eagerly.

'Then let's start there,' I suggested, and called to the pup, who largely ignored me.

As I unfolded Alban's map of the city and tore off in the direction of the library — a place which had, I freely admit, haunted my dreams for weeks — I was too aware of the swarming infestation of ortherex parasites heaving and churning somewhere beneath my feet. While I knew they posed little threat to me or my present companions, their presence added nothing to my comfort. Apart from anything, they *looked* repulsive, and that, however unfairly, is often enough to incite disgust. Just think of how un-popular spiders are, even the ones that can cause no harm whatsoever.

And then, the fact that they'd apparently eaten an entire city did little to endear them to me.

I tried not to think about them, other than to keep some of our driving questions at the forefront of my thoughts: what had brought them here? How and why had they stayed?

'Ves,' Jay called, interrupting my thoughts.

'Mm?' I looked up, and was treated to a view of an unfamiliar street. Human-sized dwellings predominated there, most of them built from a mixture of reddish brick and timber: I'd wandered into a row of merchant's houses, I judged, or something like that.

Which was lovely, but not exactly to the point.

Do you know, I reckon this is why I can find nothing and nowhere. I might set off in the right direction, but then my mind wanders and I stop paying attention to where I am, where I've been, and where I'm supposed to be going.

Sheepishly, I retraced my steps and handed the map to someone with less of a fatal tendency to daydream, otherwise known as Jay.

He was kind enough not to rib me about it this time, or maybe he was just too focused on the mission. Like I was supposed to be.

I sighed.

He got us to the library steps within minutes. I trotted along with my shields up and my head in the clouds; Rob kept wary eyes on the velvety, lightning-laced sky; Indira moved like a woman on a mission, exhibiting all the laser-like focus I wish I had.

'Stop,' said Jay as we mounted the steps. 'Something's different here.'

Perhaps it was no surprise that it was me who noticed it first. 'Colours,' I said, elegantly terse — or fatuously unhelpful, depending on your point of view. I gestured at the long, long windows set into the front of the soaring, white-stone building before us. They were filled in with leaded lights: many small, diamond-shaped panes of glass fitted edge-to-edge. Previously the glass had been clear. Now, they were a wash of dazzling, rainbow colour through which a soft light shone. 'I'd swear these weren't stained glass before.'

'Or lit up like a Christmas tree,' said Jay.

Indira, to my confusion, squatted down right there in the street and laid a palm against one pale stone slab. 'These are warm,' she said thoughtfully.

'Is that significant?' I wasn't catching her drift.

'Might be.' She paused there in thought for a moment, then rose gracefully and re-joined us.

I noticed that Rob had drawn his lovely, terrifying silvered knives.

I also noticed that Ms. Goodfellow seemed to be having a *very* good time, though I could not determine why. Always a bundle of energy (except when comatose), she'd begun running in circles, a frenzy in miniature, her ears and tail flying. 'Pause,' I said to her, and scooped her up. Retrieving my hair-changing ring from her horn again (how did she keep doing that?), I gave her a swift sanity check.

She stared up at me with liquid eyes, tongue lolling in a canine grin.

'You're mad,' I told her. 'But I suppose that's not so unusual.'

Jay had, cautiously, approached the main doors of the library, which opened to welcome him. The moment I set the pup down, she shot inside, yapping.

'We should be careful—' Rob was saying. He broke off with a sigh. 'Okay, we can do it that way.' He went after her, a silvery knife glinting in one fist and the Lapis Wand in the other.

Jay, Indira and I followed.

Something had changed inside, too. The air thrummed, a sound I might have connected with something like a central heating system if we weren't standing in a building that far predated such modern conceits. What's more, something was happening to the floor. I stepped out of my shoes, and soon saw what Indira had been talking about: the coloured tiles underfoot, which should have been cool, were toasty warm, and faintly pulsing.

I extracted my favourite book from his sleeping bag. 'Mauf. You awake?'

'Yes, madam.'

'Did you ever experience anything like this before? Or your predecessor, I suppose. Did he? Any pertinent memories?'

'I have not the pleasure of understanding you.'

'The colours, the lights, the heat,' I elaborated.

'My predecessor (as you term him) having spent the greater part of three centuries blissfully insensate, I am afraid I can be of little assistance. The library certainly was not known to display such unseemly exuberance in those earlier days, when he found it possible to be awake.' I detected a note of disdain. It was not the first time Mauf had displayed some little hostility towards the prototype of a book upon which he had been modelled.

'Does Lady Tregawny say anything about such phenomenon?' I hoped he'd had sufficient time to slurp up the contents of her memoirs by then.

'Not a word.'

That might mean her ladyship's memoirs predated these peculiarities, or it may mean merely that she had never had cause to discuss them. 'Thanks,' I remembered to say, my mind busy.

I went to stash him again, but he leapt in my hands and actually began to vibrate. 'Wait! You promised.'

'So I did. Come on, then.' Avoiding the chamber nearest the main doors, from which spot Jay had originally snagged his predecessor, I followed Rob into a different chamber. This one was airy and light, a clear dome arcing over the ceiling. Spotless, of course; presumably the Sweeping Symphony had cleared away any dust that might previously have accumulated.

Mauf made a kittenish growl of pleasure. 'Such erudition,' he said dreamily.

'Knock yourself out,' I told him, and set him on a low table that stood between two towering bookcases. As yet, Pup had not re-materialised and I was becoming anxious about her. 'Goodie?' I called, uselessly. She probably did not yet understand that this dignified moniker was, approximately, her name.

But then the tick-tick of her claws upon the tiled floor alerted me to her approach, and she came bounding around a corner. She made for me at a flat run, hurtling headlong in my general direction, jaws fixed in a huge smile.

She had a jewelled scroll-case lodged between her teeth.

'How lovely,' I said, wincing as she collided with my legs. 'Is it useful, Pup, or just pretty?'

'Hey,' said Jay from somewhere nearby. I couldn't see him. '*Some* would argue that a thing may be both pretty and useful, no?'

I vaguely recognised one of my own maxims being repeated back to me there, and stuck out my tongue, forgetting that he could not see me either.

I wrestled the case from Goodie Goodfellow and tried to prise it open, but its ends were sealed fast and wouldn't budge.

When, a moment later, a babble of voices abruptly cut through the prevailing quiet, coming from somewhere two or three rooms away, I mumbled a garbled curse and stuffed the case into my satchel. Jay was way ahead of me; I almost collided with him as I tore in the direction of the inexplicable tumult. Rob had gone that way.

We found him standing in the middle of a room I'd never seen before, a far larger chamber than the rest of the library. Its central hall, I surmised, for it had the cathedral-like height and splendid vaulting that might suit such an important spot. A smooth starstone floor stretched away into the near distance, inset with gilded curlicued ornaments, and — like the library at Mandridore — silvery puffs of cloud hung where the ceiling ought to be. There were fewer books here, and no actual bookcases. Instead, sections of the stone walls were covered over with glass, and behind the glass hung artefacts of, no doubt, unspeakable rarity and power. Most of them were great, gilt-edged tomes with ornate hinges, or — my heart sank a bit — scrolls in jewelled cases, awfully like the one the dear pup had just surrendered into my care.

The voices were coming from some of the books.

'Giddy gods,' I breathed. 'More chatty tomes?'

'I think,' said Indira cautiously, 'this is different.'

I saw her point. Unlike Mauf (or indeed Bill), who spoke like he had a mind stuffed somewhere into his bindings, these books were shrieking the same words over and over, like trained parrots. *It burns us, it hurts us, take it away!* yelled an otherwise sober-looking book in a black binding.

We told you, we said so, we knew how it would be! repeated another, jauntier tome, flashing richly-coloured interior illuminations as it danced in agitation.

They weren't all distressed, however. *Lovely, lovely, lovely, lovely,* sang a little jade-coloured book, and I developed an immediate desire to take it home with us. *It's time, it's time, how we've missed it!* chortled another.

A scroll in a ruby-studded jacket simply cackled without cease.

'Farringale's lunatic asylum for books?' suggested Jay, backing away a step.

'Are they mad?' I mused. 'Or just really pepped up?'

'I'm not sure "pep" is a word I'd use,' said Jay. 'Except maybe for that one.' He waved a hand at the giggling scroll.

I turned and left the cacophonic hallway at a run. 'I think we're going to need Mauf.'

16

By the time I returned, two of the beleaguered books had begun beating themselves against the walls of their glass-fronted houses. Whether they were trying to escape, or merely entertaining themselves, was unclear.

'Mauf,' I yelled over the tumult. 'What is going on here?'

'They appear to be in a state of some excitement,' said Mauf gravely.

'*Yes,* I can see that, but why? Can you talk to them?'

'I would as usefully talk to a wall. A more empty-headed set of volumes I never did encounter.'

'Is that the truth, Mauf, or do you exaggerate for effect?'

'A very little exaggeration only, Miss Vesper.'

What could he mean? The word "empty-headed" must be an expression he had picked up from us, or some other book; it could not literally apply here. Were the books devoid of useful content, or were they somehow empty of words altogether?

I wanted to examine one. Unfortunately, the glass walls behind which they were imprisoned must have been mag-ickally reinforced; for all their pounding and bouncing, none had contrived to escape.

So I fetched out my Sunstone Wand, and with a flick and a whisper, sent a bolt of crackling fire at the nearest of them — which happened (entirely by chance, I swear) to be the happy-natured jade-green book.

My little fireball bounced harmlessly off the glass and fell to the stone floor, where it lay sulking and sizzling.

'Damn.'

'You want that one?' said Rob, withdrawing the Lapis Lazuli Wand from his sleeve.

'Please, and thank you.' I smiled.

He did his glass-shattering trick. I've never been able to master it. The glass imprisoning my chosen book turned ink-black, then cracked into a thousand pieces and fell away in a rain of... sand, this time.

'Ouch,' Rob grunted. 'Powerful enchantments in here.' A sheen of sweat glistened on his forehead. He frowned, and stared at the Wand as though he'd never seen it before. 'I feel like that shouldn't have worked.'

I ran and snatched up the book before it could get any bright ideas about, say, flying away, and opened it with breathless eagerness.

I saw at once what Mauf had meant.

'It's not that there aren't words,' I said, showing the pages to the others. 'But something's... happened to them.' Page after page was full of gibberish, the genuinely non-sensical kind. I didn't see a single coherent word, not in any language I knew, and besides that they were no longer arranged in the tidy rows one tended to expect. A great many letters, and in some cases whole words, had wandered off, wriggling all over the page like snails at a picnic. As I watched, some turned odd colours and faded away, then reappeared.

'It isn't some kind of code?' said Jay, but doubtfully.

'Not consistent enough, surely?' I said. 'Do you see any coherence whatsoever?'

Mauf, still tucked under my left arm, said clearly: 'Magick-addled.'

'It's what?' I said.

'Round the bend,' clarified Mauf. 'It probably gets worse every time.'

'Every time what... uh, Indira?' Something moved at the edge of my vision. I looked that way just in time to see Jay's sober and serious sister shoot into the air like a firework, her dark skirt and airy white blouse fluttering. Her hair streamed in a wind I could not feel.

While it was not unusual to see Indira levitate, and most adeptly too, this was different. For one thing, she rose and rose to at least twenty feet up, rapidly approaching those gauzy and unlikely clouds. For another thing, she was laughing in a fashion most unlike her.

'Indira?' called Jay. 'That's too high. Come down now.'

'Is that even possible?' I breathed, awed. Levitating to *twenty feet*? Actually, forget it. Indira wasn't even levitating anymore. She was flat-out flying.

'*I* never saw her do that before,' said Jay. 'Indira!'

Mauf gave what felt curiously like a bookish sigh. 'I can see you are all to become quite tiresome. Perhaps you might restore me to the other chamber? I was engaged in a most interesting conversation.'

I barely attended to this speech, for Indira was shouting something. 'There is so much of it!' she laughed. 'It's wonderful. Like drowning in chocolate.' There was more, but she became less coherent and farther away in equal measure.

The floor was thrumming again. I discarded my shoes a second time, and my socks, too, pressing my bare feet to the stones. That felt quite nice actually, so I lay down and stretched out. The low thrumming filled me, too, in soft pulses of warmth; it was like lying in the grass on a warm summer afternoon, that feeling of balmy contentment exactly, only about fifty times as potent.

I'd put myself eye-level with my useless fireball from earlier. Should it not have burned out by now? But it lay there still, spinning lazily, and emitting occasional puffs of coloured smoke.

Mauf lay near me. 'Miss Vesper,' he said. 'Far be it from me to question your choices, but might this not be an excellent time to leave?'

'No,' I said, and giggled. 'It's lovely, lovely, lovely.' The jade-green book and I sang it together, and I was distantly aware that I was smiling like an idiot — dancing, too, despite my recumbent posture — but the part of me that might normally have cared about such peculiar behaviour lay quiet and inert.

Rob sat slumped against a nearby wall. He'd stopped trying to fish Indira down and instead sat with his gaze fixed upon the clouds far above, smiling faintly. He still had the Lazuli Wand in hand; once in a while he gave it a spiralling little flourish, and some magickal thing leapt into being. A butterfly of painted silk. A tiny smoke dragon. A stream of miniature cars which roared across the floor, tooting tiny horns.

This looked like fun, so I joined in. I filled the air with dancing cakes, created a self-operating toot-organ with a taste for jazz (if you've never heard of a toot-organ, don't ask me to explain for I'm sure I cannot). I even turned myself, briefly, into a pancake, but since this caused Rob to eye me hungrily I hastily changed back.

I slowly became aware of Jay standing over me, shrouded in a mantle of smoke dragons and gyrating cakes but nonetheless, inexplicably, frowning. 'How can you be so severe,' I said to him, and with a flick of my Wand I gave him a crown of sad faces etched in light and shadow.

'Ves,' he said. 'We need to leave.' His voice was slurred, and his movements sluggish, but he spoke firmly.

'But how could we, when the furniture is so flatteringly eager for our company?' For a party of chairs from a nearby chamber had that moment come clattering in. For all their graceful construction, silken upholstery and mahogany frames, they were clumsy in their movements, and chattered in coarse voices.

'Look at that one,' said their leader, scornfully. 'Thinks it's a chaise longue, does it? I've seen better padding on my grandmother's couch.' I realised, with a start, that the chair was speaking of me, for it delivered a kick to my shin with one slender, polished leg.

'I like this one,' said another, flouncing over to Rob. 'Substantial. Firm. A chair you could trust.'

This, all told, was not an unreasonable description.

'It is of no use,' said Mauf. 'You will have to wait until the flow has ebbed.'

'The flow?' said Jay, pausing in the act of prodding my various soft parts with his toe. Not gently.

'Of magick.'

This made so much sense, I was overwhelmed by the sheer beauteous perfection of it. The possibility had entered our heads not so long ago, and now here we were experiencing something of that exact sort! I began to laugh, so delighted was I.

Jay, though, was neither so impressed nor so convinced. 'Is it magick or are they high?' he muttered, and retired to a corner.

'Both,' I tittered. 'I think.' I watched, some of my joy fading, as Jay slumped to the floor and sat with his head against the wall, his eyes closing. 'Jay! Why aren't *you* high?'

'I feel unwell,' he said shortly.

'How unfair.' I jumped to my feet. I don't know what I was planning to do — run after him and *make him* enjoy the experience? — but a powerful headrush halted me where I stood, and I swayed.

A moment later I was back on the floor again, higgledy-piggledy.

'Ouch,' said Jay, apparently his idea of sympathy.

I looked up. Indira was still flying, swan-like, some way above. As I stared, glassy-eyed, something horned and yellow-furred and puppish floated slowly past, upside down and grinning.

'You know,' I said, tightly shutting my eyes. 'Since you mention it, I'm not sure I feel so great either.' That balmy, cocooned feeling faded in a rush, leaving me breathless in its sudden absence. Instead I felt squeezed, as though a great weight pressed down on me. Energy surged up from the floor, from the walls, from the very air, jolting through me like pulses of lightning; every hair on my body rose, and I began hyperventilating with the effort to breathe. I couldn't sit still. I was too much of a livewire for that.

I thought I heard, as from a great distance, the voice of Mauf screaming, 'Purple-hued malt-worm!'

All of this sounds terrifying, doesn't it? Only, it wasn't. I felt exhilarated, like I could jump out of a plane — or, perhaps, like I just had. I felt more alive than I ever remembered feeling before; and when, some unmeasurable time later, the energies washed out of me like the tide and left me empty, I felt bereft and diminished.

I sat, quiet and listless, as details of my surroundings slowly filtered through to my befuddled consciousness. Mauf lay tutting a few feet away. 'I *told* you to leave,' he muttered darkly. Our purloined jade-green book had ended up stuffed up my shirt; I had no memory of putting it there, and hastily retrieved it. It had ceased to chortle, or to speak, and lay unmoving in my hand, somehow seeming to weigh twice as much as it had before.

Rob sat still against the wall, blinking and shaking his head. Jay I could not see, nor Indira — until both came hurtling into view together, falling at ill-advised speed from the heavens.

They landed with a *crunch*.

'Ouch,' I said.

Jay groaned.

'I was *fine*,' said Indira waspishly as she picked herself up.

Jay just lay there, grimacing. 'You wouldn't have been in another five minutes.'

He had a point. To my dismay, all of Rob's smoke drag-ons and butterflies were dissolving into dust and winking away. My cake chorus was already gone, and I no longer felt either the desire or the capacity to turn myself into a giant pancake.

Whoever would've thought I'd ever say that last bit with such gravity, or with such regret?

I got up, and upon finding myself generally stable I went over to Jay, and hauled upon his arm until he righted him-self. 'Anything broken?'

'Not for lack of trying.'

I looked at Indira. 'So how many times have you broken a limb?'

'Three,' she said, unblinking. 'Why do you ask?'

'Oh, no reason.'

Jay snorted.

I retrieved Mauf, and then Goodie, who I found stranded upon a shelf some six feet from the floor. I had not imagined the part about the flying Dappledok pup, then. Had I imagined any of it? No. Jay wasn't wrong to use the word *high,* for we'd certainly lost touch with a few useful things like rationality and common sense. But we hadn't been hallucinating.

I tried to remember when I had ever heard of such a surge happening before, or any similar effects if it had. Nothing came to mind — except, of course, the storyteller's tale on Whitmore. 'The Seas of Segorne,' I mused aloud.

'And the Vales of Wonder,' said Jay.

Seeing Rob and Indira wearing twin expressions of confusion, I explained. 'We heard a rumour on Whitmore. They said that the last king of Farringale — *our* Farringale, that is, so Torvaston the Second — escaped to the Fifth Britain with an entourage. And they went looking for places prone to excesses of magick.'

'But no,' said Indira, frowning. 'Torvaston and Hrruna founded the new court at Mandridore.'

'So the history books say, but they've been wrong before.'

Indira looked appalled, as well she might, studious girl that she was. The only comfort I could offer was a pat on the arm. 'History's a changeful beast. It's one of the exhilarating things about it.'

'Crushing and exhilarating,' said Jay darkly.

'Utterly crushing.'

'But why wouldn't Torvaston go to Mandridore?' said Indira.

'This is one of the questions we're here trying to answer,' I said. 'The Troll Court had nothing about Torvaston, and precious little about the early days of Mandridore.'

'Nothing at all?'

'Not even a scrawled note.'

'But that means...'

'It means the story may have a kernel of truth to it. And Torvaston must have had a really solid reason for fleeing into the fifth instead of going with his wife.'

'Like?' That was Rob. He'd listened in silence up until then, but his grim face suggested that his thoughts were running along similar lines to mine.

'It's only a hypothesis, yet,' I said cautiously. 'But I've wondered before. What could possibly compel Torvaston to abandon his wife, his people, his court, and flee? And what could motivate him to go looking for dangerously magick-drunk places like the Seas of Segorne? Jay, I think you might be right. I think they were expelled from the Court — because they were addicted to magick.'

Rob nodded.

'Magick-drunk,' Indira repeated. 'You mean it literally.'

'It *was* fun, wasn't it?' I said, with a small smile. 'I could get used to having that much magick around myself. I think the Court of Farringale did, too — or some of them, at least. Jay is proof that not everyone's as deeply suscepti-ble to the allure, but... such things have happened before. What might you do, if you needed your fix but there wasn't enough around?'

'Surely not,' said Rob. 'You mean to say *Torvaston* flooded Farringale?'

'Yes,' I said, utterly serious. 'That's exactly what I think happened.'

17

'Farringale destroyed by its own king,' said Jay, and whistled. 'That would be reason enough to expel him from Mandridore, certainly.'

'And to cover the whole thing up afterwards,' I agreed. 'I'm sure Hrruna wouldn't have wanted her husband to be remembered that way.'

'So they went off into the Vales of Wonder looking for a new source,' said Rob. 'And the excess of magick attracted the ortherex, who feed off some derivative of it; and they're still here. It fits, Ves, but do you have any evidence for it?'

'We're working on that.'

Indira was shaking her head, though she did not speak.

'What's on your mind?' I prompted.

'Surely...' she said. 'Surely no king would ever make such destructive decisions. And Torvaston is spoken of as a wise leader.'

'I don't imagine he made any such decision consciously, or rationally. But who decides to become an alcoholic? It is the kind of thing that happens by slow degrees, usually driven by some other factor. Perhaps Torvaston was feeling the pressures of leadership. Farringale was, after all, the most powerful and famous of the Fae Courts at the time. He might find himself turning more and more to something that eased the pressure, made him feel better. Some of his courtiers might follow suit.' I knew my ideas bordered upon treasonous, or they might be if I was a subject of Their Majesties myself. It's why I had opted not to mention any of my thoughts to Alban. Nor would I, until I had sound evidence to support them. 'Or it may have been unintentional. If I could turn myself into a pancake and Indira could fly, what else could you do with that much magick? What if they were trying to achieve something truly stupendous, and it got out of hand?'

'But how?' said Jay. 'How does a magick-drunk king flood an entire city?'

'Right. Top question. We need to find the source of magick for Farringale Dell and get a good look at it. I'm thinking it might be possible to draw on it, in some way, or to goose it — I don't know. Magick is too weak in modern

Britain to pose any such problems. I doubt anyone's been magick-drunk in decades, if not centuries.'

'If they have,' said Jay, 'it's been as adroitly covered up as Torvaston's fall.'

A sobering thought. The Hidden Ministry was, after all, dedicated to keeping magickal secrets — besides being rather a secret itself. *Had* something like this happened more recently? I should call Mabyn, at the Forbidden Magick department. If it had, maybe she would know.

But, priorities. 'Mauf,' I said. 'Lady Tregawny's memoirs. This is why I brought them. Does she speak of anything that sounds like it might be the magickal heart of Farringale Dell?'

'Not as such,' said Mauf, but he spoke hesitantly. 'She was writing a little before Torvaston's day, of course, but she writes of a festival at midsummer. It was held only once every five or so years. *We processed out of the City and into the Dell, my fellowes and I, garbed in festive raiment and all of a tumult, with our Gaiety and our Song. Their Majesties went ahead of us, as is Their Wont, and equally Their Right; and we of the Lesser Court did not reach the summit for some hours. When at last our moment came, so spongy was I that forward I went, hugger-mugger, and swounded quite away. 'Gramercy,' said I when once more I was myself, for despite my unseemly weakness they had allotted me a fair draught...'*

'Spongy?' I said, befuddled.

'Drunk,' Mauf supplied.

'Perhaps she meant inebriated in the ordinary sense,' said Jay. 'But if she did, what is the "fair draught"? It hardly makes sense for it to be some kind of beverage, or why did they go out into the Dell for it?'

'And the summit?' put in Rob. 'Of what, and why were they going there?'

'She does not say, in any greater detail than I have already shared,' said Mauf.

'Why would she?' I said. 'She was describing a familiar ritual. One headed up by Their Majesties and their Court...' Something about the word *summit* nagged at me.

'There is a mountain,' offered Indira in her quiet way. 'I saw it.' Rather than add any more words to her sentence, she pointed upwards. She'd seen it when she was flying.

And that reminded me. 'There *is* a mountain somewhere out there,' I said excitedly. 'Alban mentioned it when we first came here. He said that, according to legend, it was so tall that its peak touched the clouds. It's where the griffins are supposed to have nested. Maybe that's the source! The festival! You said five years *or so*, Mauf. It wasn't every five years precisely?'

'Lady Tregawny implies that the dates were variable,' said Mauf. 'In the year she speaks of, the festival came upon them apparently by surprise.'

'So it was early!' I was growing excited, for everything was falling into place in my mind. 'Don't you see? These magickal surges had been happening for a while, but only rarely — approximately once every five years. But even by Lady Tregawny's time, some years before Torvaston, they were becoming more frequent. When they were rare, they could be celebrated and enjoyed. But when they became more common, they'd soon become disruptive and alarming. If the Court was in the habit of drawing heavily upon these surges when they came, like binge drinkers on a Saturday night, couldn't that easily get out of control? Couldn't some people end up taking far too much?'

'If that's the case,' said Rob, 'maybe it was not Torvaston who flooded Farringale.'

'He and his courtiers might have hurried the process along,' I argued. '*Something* changed a welcomed and celebrated event into a catastrophe. We need to find that mountain.'

Rob raised a hand. 'Slow down, Ves. Think. If the mountain was as tall as all that, how were so many people reaching the summit?'

'I've just spent three and a half minutes as a pancake.'

'I take your point. Indira, where is this mountain?'

This simple question puzzled clever Indira more than it ought. She took her time in answering. 'A long way off,' she said. 'And at the same time, very close. I cannot say... I think my perceptions were disordered.'

'We were all a little disordered,' said Rob kindly.

'Then again, maybe not,' I said. 'Indira just pulled a great fairy routine, and Ms. Goodfellow was both airborne and upside down.'

Rob, Indira and Jay looked at me blankly. 'What point are you making?' said Jay.

'Nothing *else* made sense for that period of time. Why should a mere immoveable landmark prove unaffected? Perhaps it *was* both near and far away. I suspect that reaching it might not be so simple as walking to it.'

'So, then,' said Jay, folding his arms. 'We find the unfindable mountain, climb its unclimbably tall peak, and see if we can get ourselves magick-drunk enough to fall off again?'

'Well.' I blinked. 'Except for maybe that last part, yes.'

'Is anything ever going to be simple around you?'

'Around me, no. But if you ask Milady nicely, she might assign you a quieter duty. You'd excel at rare books. That's usually about trawling the non-magicker libraries for misplaced spell tomes and the like. Rarely gets exciting. Or you could maybe—'

'Not serious, Ves.'

'Oh.'

Rob, damn him, was hiding a grin with very little success. Even Indira looked amused, somewhere behind her mask of composure.

'Let's get a move on,' I said hastily. 'Mauf, we need a clue. Does Lady Tregawny give any hints as to where the procession started off from, or what route they took?'

'I am afraid not, Miss Vesper.'

'There might be something else, somewhere in here,' said Indira, turning in a circle to take in the full extent of the enormous library.

'Maybe,' I agreed. 'The first problem is finding it. The second... well, I don't know that we'd find an A-to-Z Manual of Magickal Surge Festivities or anything like that. Nobody writes dreary tomes about birthday parties or stag dos for the same reason. We all know our own traditions too well to need instruction on the basics. We learn it growing up.'

'Mr. Maufry,' said Indira. 'There is nothing about the mountain, I suppose?'

'If I had a week to search...' said Mauf.

We could have stayed for a week, if we had needed to. That possibility was why I had brought things like the porridge-pot along. But who wanted to spend a whole week sitting around in the biggest, best and most beautiful library on the planet, reading book after book after book after… all right, I did. I do. But not right then, and not if I had to do it on a steady diet of porridge. Those joys could wait until after we'd restored Farringale to habitability.

Ha, ha. Said I confidently, as though there weren't about a thousand obstacles to get past in the process.

Ves. Focus!

For some reason, I'm starting to hear those words in Jay's voice. I do not know what this means.

'For once,' I said, breaking in upon a debate between Indira and her brother as to the likelihood of a useful book's being unearthed inside of a week. 'I mean, I never thought I would say this, but: I don't think books are the answer here.'

'Not?' Jay was incredulous.

'Not.'

'Are you the real Ves?'

'I'm the Ves who recently spent three splendid minutes as a pancake. You decide.'

'I withdraw the question.'

'Thank you. I think Mauf and Rob were right: we shouldn't spend too long here while these surges are going on.'

'Did I say that?' objected Rob.

'I could see you thinking it, several times. And it's true. We don't know how often these surges are going to happen, and they could be dangerous. Last time, the Patels al-

most broke three or four limbs apiece and I seriously considered spending the rest of my life as a perfectly-cooked
breakfast dish. A few more doses of that, and who knows
what could happen? We should finish up our immediate
business and get out.'

'I concur,' said cautious Jay, not at all to my surprise.

'Fine. So we do not have time to spend a week searching
the library. Which means! It's time to play Trial and Error.'

'Oh god.' Jay actually backed away from me.

'It'll be fine.'

'Are we still pretending the griffins don't exist?'

'Er.' To be truthful, I had forgotten them a bit. Their
habit of lurking (at least by report) right at the top of the
very peak we were aiming for was a tad bit inconvenient.

However.

'We've survived them before. Let's go.' I scooped up
Mauf, the happy jade-green book and Ms. Goodfellow,
stuffing all three into my satchel (well, the books anyway. I
placed my pup into her sleep-nest with tender care). Then
I marched out of the great, marble hall in the direction of
the exit.

Behind me, I heard a great, weary sigh from Jay. 'Ves. It's
this way.'

'Right.'

In the end, we made Indira lead, which did not at all make her happy. But she was the only one of us who had yet set eyes upon this mountain.

Not that it helped much. She headed off confidently enough when we regained the street, but soon faltered and became confused. 'The problem is,' she said, 'I received no clear impression of its direction from my former vantage-point. And it is deceptive.'

'Vantage-point,' I mused. 'Right. Rob, Jay, would you fetch us some of those chatty chairs?'

'On it.' Rob dived back into the library with Jay at his heels.

'Except not the rude one,' I called after them. 'The one that insulted my padding?'

They returned with two chairs apiece, and set them all before me. It was my very great pleasure to witch them up in a trice, and I say that because it was shockingly easy. Apparently I was still fizzing with magick.

No wonder people got addicted to it.

'Hup,' I said, hurling myself into the arms of the nearest chair. I'd chosen one with a wide seat and a thick cushion: space enough for my all-important satchel.

Up we went. There was a movement recently to mandate the use of seat-belts in all airborne apparatus, chairs included, which was thankfully shouted down, but I began to see their point when a gust of air almost upended my chair and me with it.

'Be advised,' I called down, my heart all a-pound. 'Playful currents up here.'

'To say the least,' said Jay, rising unsteadily to my approximate level.

I turned my chair in a slow circle, and received a dazzling view of the city laid out before me like a bejewelled chess board. Its layout was not dissimilar, vaguely grid-like, with the dappled lights and darks of sturdy buildings, though the roads curved and wound their way sinuously in between.

Beyond the confines of the city spread the rest of Farringale Dell: lusciously forested, and interspersed here and there with clear, sparkling lakes. Perhaps some part of it had once been tamed and inhabited; if so, those days were long gone. The forest had reclaimed the Dell, and begun to encroach upon the streets of the city, too.

I saw no mountain.

Then, suddenly, I did. It shimmered into view, cresting the sea of broad-leaved trees like some kind of desert mirage. 'There!' I shouted, pointing excitedly. Clouds swirled around the peak, as advertised, lightning shooting in crackling golden coils. Griffins, presumably, lurked somewhere within.

I became aware that my announcement had not caused quite the sensation I'd expected. As I was trying to bounce out of my chair with excitement, Jay was doing the same not far away — only he was waving his arm in a different direction altogether.

So was Rob.

So was Indira.

'Wait, wait,' I said, and brought my chair to a hovering halt. 'There cannot be four such mountains.'

Even as I said the words, a voice at the back of my mind said: *Whyever not?*

'No!' I said, smothering it. 'Don't be ridiculous. Only one can be real.'

'Or none,' said Jay.

'Right. Where then is the real one?'

18

INDIRA HAD FLOWN HIGHER, much higher. I stared up at the distant underside of her elegant chair with some concern. Given her propensity for shattering bones, I didn't want to end up taking her home in several pieces. 'Indira?' I called.

'Give her a moment,' said Jay.

Well, if Jay didn't feel like being older-brother-protective, far be it from me to play Mother Hen. I waited, my thoughts busy.

If Jay was right and all four mountains were illusory: why? And what was causing it? We each saw only one mountain, which meant we were each being fed a separate vision. By... something. Well, by the mountain. If it was indeed the source of magick for Farringale Dell, what might it not be capable of?

But why did it wish to hide itself?

'If you were an age-old magickal mountain with a penchant for griffin headgear, where and why might you hide?' I said.

Rob, having positioned himself directly below Indira, did not answer. Catching our youngest team member if she happened to plummet to her inevitable death seemed like a great priority to me, so I didn't interrupt him.

'For some reason, I'm having trouble fitting myself into the headspace of a rock-based landmark.' Jay kept a close eye on Indira, too, which might not have been helping his focus.

Focus, focus. Hm.

How about if I stopped thinking of it as a mountain? Perhaps more importantly, it was (if we were right) a magickal... font, I suppose. Terms vary for such things, and we don't truly understand them very well. To call the heart of a magickal Dell a "font" likens it to some kind of fountain, merrily pumping out magick all the livelong day, and that's in no way an accurate idea. You can't switch it on or off, like a tap. But Dells — capital D, because they really are markedly different from your common-or-garden dingle — grow up around such a source. It's what makes them magickal, and sets them apart. It's rare, but once in a while a Dell falters and dies, because its source fails. We still have no idea why. I'd been inclined to think it a consequence of the decline of magick, but we'd since learned that it happened on the fifth Britain, too, so that idea was out.

In this instance, we had the opposite problem going on. That this occurred on the fifth Britain was no surprise whatsoever; the place was bursting with magick. But for it to happen here? Different situation entirely. The Heart of Farringale Dell was in no danger of drying up; on the contrary it was prone to giving rather too freely of itself. And its former citizens had been disposed to celebrate the fact.

First point, then: did I believe that the entire Court of Farringale would go tramping many miles through forest and dale to reach this magickal mountain, on the occasion of their festival? No. They could have flown, of course, as we were doing, but that would take a *lot* of chairs, and anyway, nothing about Lady Tregawny's memoirs had implied she might have been airborne for any part of it. Had they all flown, like Indira? Probably not, but maybe. Even if they had, how far could a swarm of people safely fly, even pumped up on magick?

So that suggested the mountain was situated not too far from the city, or (more sensibly) vice versa.

Right, then.

'Indira!' I yelled. 'You're my spotter.'

'What?' The word floated faintly back to me on the wind.

'You see anything move, *scream.*'

'Ves,' yelled Jay. 'What are you doing?'

This I ignored. Not because I was indifferent to my partner's concern but because I was a bit busy.

Step one: I summoned up the strongest wards I had, and cloaked all four of us in them. I added a splash of camouflage into them this time. Whether it would help much in the circumstances I did not know, but it couldn't hurt.

Step two: I wafted a little higher, and began a wide circle of the city. In one hand I had my Sunstone Wand; in the other, my syrinx pipes.

I took the precaution of laying a gentle sleep-spell on the pup before I began. I didn't want her leaping out of the chair.

The melody I chose was a mixture of two distinct things: the first being the pacifying charm I had employed on our last visit to Farringale, and the second pure siren call. I've put a lot of time and practice into the art of pipe-playing and music-based magick over the past decade or so. You do, when you're unexpectedly put in possession of a great Treasure and even permitted to keep it. My music soared over Farringale, haunting and alluring and calming all at the same time.

'You're a madwoman, Ves!' shouted Jay, but I felt him join his magick to mine even as he spoke. The music gained in both intensity and volume, enough to spread to every corner of Farringale Dell.

'You got a better idea?' I yelled back.

I thought I heard a distant chuckle from Rob, but it may have been a trick of the wind.

Indira spotted something. Perhaps it wasn't movement, for there was a distinct lack of screaming. Instead she raised one slim arm in the air, Wand in hand, and sent a burst of scintillating light flying high into the sky, like a flare. The light split and spread and poured down again, swirling chaotically around an apparently featureless stretch of dappled green-and-golden trees.

'Gotcha,' I muttered, and veered that way. My chair shot through the skies at dangerous speed by then; wind whipped into my face, stinging my skin, and the cold threatened to numb my lips.

As soon as I drew near to the rosy-lit trees, I began to see why Indira had lit them up. A suppressed shimmer of magick lay under every leaf, and when I got within twenty feet or so the trees themselves wavered like water.

You'd think this would have been warning enough. In my defence, I was probably moving too fast to stop in time anyway. Intent upon the maintenance of my rippling melody, I angled my chair in between the broad trunks of two ancient trees — and they disappeared in a flash. What I saw instead was the rugged, rocky expanse of an undeniably solid mountain rising steep and sharp before me.

I had about two and a half seconds to admire the view before I collided with it. The *crunch* was sickening.

I lay, spread-eagled and dazed, among the wreckage of my poor chair, blessing the shields which had — slightly — cushioned the fall. I only blazed with hurt *almost* everywhere.

'Pup?' I croaked, and groped for my satchel. Ms. Goodfellow came crawling out, and curled up upon my stomach.

'Good,' I gasped, and returned my pipes to my lips. I don't know if you've ever tried playing a wind instrument when all the wind has just been smartly knocked out of you, but it isn't easy.

Jay came bombing into view. Being forewarned, courtesy of Ves, he did not repeat my graceless performance but landed with a crisp *snap* and leapt out of his chair. 'How the hell is it that you manage to keep *not being dead*?' he said, at (I thought) unreasonable volume.

I waved a hand at him in a *hush, you* gesture. 'They're coming,' I said, removing the pipes but briefly from my lips.

'Who are— oh my god.' A shadow passed over the sun; Jay looked up, and up, and stood mouth agape, for soaring overhead was a magickal beast straight out of legend. The size of a small ship, with a lion's body and a bird's plumage, it was mottled in white and tawny-yellow and red, its body wreathed in crackling lightning. Its beak was shut, talons peacefully curled as it spiralled its lazy way down to where I and my pipes lay.

Another two came wafting down behind it.

Considering that, last time, we'd been greeted with sharp beaks and claws, I thought this something of an improvement.

But Jay stood rigid as a rock, until the first griffin landed barely five feet away and he began to tremble. 'Uh,' he whispered, and apparently ran out of words.

I couldn't blame him. I make it a point of honour never to visibly lose my shit, but it was difficult not to. The last time I had been in close quarters with a griffin, it had been trying to eat my face. Easily thirty times my size, this one was passive only because I played. Probably? What would happen if I ran out of breath?

Rob. Rob would happen. A dark shape flitted across the sky not far from the majestic griffins; Rob was ready, his enchanted knives in hand, to get those blades between me and the griffin if necessary.

Keep it together, Ves, I told myself. I didn't want us to die that day, but I didn't want any griffins to die that day either.

'Ves,' said Indira, very softly, from behind me. I jumped. I hadn't seen or heard her approach. 'Ves, you can stop playing.'

I leaned back my head, and signalled with my eyes that she was insane.

She smiled faintly. 'No, really. It's all right. Stop.'

Returning my wary gaze to the nearest of the three griffins, I tentatively let my song trail off. The melody continued without me, its volume a little muted, but the enchantment held.

'The rocks have got it,' said Indira.

Of course they did. 'Right,' I said, and, very carefully, sat up, resettling my unhappy pup in my lap. 'You realise you two could rule the world if you wanted to?' I added, addressing Indira and Jay.

'Some other time,' said Jay tightly.

'Where did you get those pipes?' said Indira.

I considered trotting out the line I'd used on Jay (*classified, sorry*), which was true enough, but I felt I owed Indira for the rocks thing. 'Got them from a unicorn,' I said nonchalantly.

Jay eyeballed me. 'Of course you did. Would this be a good time to enquire what we're doing playing chicken with a trio of griffins?'

'We're getting a good look at everything.'

'Everything?'

'Mountain plus occupants.' I made a go-on motion with my hands.

Jay gave a slightly shaky sigh, and squared his shoulders. 'Should've been a librarian,' he muttered under his breath.

Indira, however, was already way ahead of him. And, for that matter, me. 'It's not the mountain,' she said softly.

"It", I supposed, meant the magickal heart of Farringale Dell, and she was right. It was a shapely and attractive mountain, to be sure, and all aflourish, but it was no magick-soaked source of one of the most potent Dells in history.

The griffins, though. Those were highly interesting.

Back in the mid thirteen hundreds, a fine fellow named Sir John Mandeville wrote a travel memoir. Val has a prized early edition in the original French, which no one — *no one* — is permitted to go near. In this wondrous volume, he describes the griffin thus (loosely translated): "...*Some men say they have the body upward as an eagle and beneath as a lion; and truly they say sooth, that they be of that shape. But one griffin hath the body more great and is more strong than eight lions, of such lions as be on this half, and more great and stronger than an hundred eagles such as we have amongst us...*" I'd now say even this princely description rather understated the case. Eight lions? Maybe triple that number, and... keep going.

They were mesmerising, terrifying, awe-inspiring — and they radiated magick. They had so much of it they couldn't hold it; hence the gold-touched lightning that rippled and flickered ceaselessly over their glossy feathers, even when they stood, heads drooping, gently at rest.

I risked a quick glance upwards. We had attracted three. How many more were up there?

'Is it the *griffins*?' I said in awe. 'Are they the heart of Farringale?'

19

'I THINK SO,' WHISPERED Indira, gazing at our griffin companion like a woman ensorcelled.

If true, the implications were astounding. It has long been supposed that magickal beasts are drawn to the magick that soaks every inch of a Dell or Enclave. What if, sometimes, it was the other way around? What if it was the *beasts* who brought the magick to the Dells? Or some combination of the two?

We'd let griffins die out. They'd been hunted for their claws and horns and bones: "For he hath his talons so long and so large and great upon his feet, as though they were horns of great oxen or of bugles or of kine, so that men make cups of them to drink of. And of their ribs and of the pens of their wings, men make bows, full strong, to shoot with arrows and quarrels." (Mandeville again).

Their talons and feathers and eggs were said to have various restorative or curative properties, and perhaps that was even the truth. There was also the incidental fact that they could be somewhat dangerous. For all these reasons and more, they had been hunted to destruction centuries ago.

A chagrined thought drifted across my mind. If magick had declined, was this partly why? We'd been killing off some of its most potent sources for the sake of a feather or two.

I'm occasionally ashamed to classify myself as human.

One of the griffins was staring right at me.

I managed not to squeak, and I was proud of myself for that small victory. The griffin in question might have been the smallest of the three, but that was not saying much. It could still have swallowed me in a single *snap* of its beak.

I stared back.

Those eyes, the deep green of fresh moss, held a spark of liveliness I found surprising considering the potency of my magickal lullaby. All right, maybe it was arrogance to think my own mere magicks could hold a trio of griffins for more than three seconds. But I *had* got those pipes from a creature of similar magickal eminence, which said a lot for their efficacy; and it had worked before, when I had almost been swallowed by one.

This griffin, though, was definitely not lulled. Nor was it making violent objection to our foray into its territory.

It looked like... dared I believe it? Like it was not so much tranquillised by the music as simply... enjoying it.

'Well,' Jay croaked. 'If you're right about this lot, it's just possible they won't eat us.'

Indeed. Because according to Lady Tregawny, the population of Farringale had made festive pilgrimages out here to the griffins' mountain in order to... what, exactly? Our new hypothesis cast her account in a different light. *They had allotted me a fair draught...* what had they been doing? Were they celebrating those surges of magick, or — or making use of them?

Especially Torvaston.

'Considering we are the first people to set foot in Farringale for quite some years—' I began.

'As far as we know,' put in Jay.

I inclined my head in acknowledgement of this point. 'Their earlier aggression may have had more to do with surprise than a deep-seated need to rend us apart.'

'They can't be the same ones as were here in Torvaston's day,' Jay said, shaking his head.

'Can't? Do you know how long griffins live?'

'No,' he allowed. 'How long do they live?'

'I'm not sure anyone knows. We kept killing them for their feathers.'

Jay grimaced. 'Right.'

Something unpleasant was happening to the floor. I'd become aware of it first as a faint warmth, and then a low, peaceful, thrumming, as of nectar-drunk bees.

Then the ground began to pulse, slowly, rhythmically, like a heartbeat.

It *was* a heartbeat. The goldish lightning crackled and buzzed around the three griffins, whose lassitude fell away. Soon, all three wore sheet lightning like cloaks, and the jolts of energy made my teeth buzz.

I realised what was happening, but too late.

'This is going to hurt,' I gasped, and was all too swiftly proved right.

PERHAPS HALF AN HOUR later, the four of us lay, felled like little trees, alone upon the mountainside. Our griffin "friends" had gone.

Okay, they had left us intact, and that was nice. But they had used us like some kind of magickal dumping-ground and that I did *somewhat* resent.

Despite my weakness, Lady Tregawny had said, and that, too, suddenly made sense. If you pumped a frail witch full of this much magick, she might not *swound* so much as suffer a heart attack on the spot. How fortunate that her ladyship had survived the experience long enough to write about it.

I tried to speak, but only a strangled choking sound emerged.

Rob began to cough. I'm pretty sure somebody else vomited, but I could not tell who.

'Right,' I managed, after another minute or so of deep breathing. 'Let's turn this to good effect, shall we?'

'How?' gasped Jay.

'First, I'm going to need my chair back.' I staggered to my feet, and limped over to the broken remains of my little vehicle. My technique was poor, I'll give you that. I merely rammed lumps of wood roughly together and welded them there by pure force of will and magick. The result was as graceless as I so often was, which seemed fitting. Plus, I enjoyed a fractional lessening of the teeming magick that soaked my every pore.

Jay was getting into the spirit of things. 'I want some more books,' he said faintly, having managed to clamber into his own chair.

'The shiny ones,' I mumbled. 'In the glass.'

'Yep. Those.'

'And then we are getting out of here,' said Rob, sternly. 'I think we've had enough fun at the Farringale party for today.'

The way I felt just then — like a wrung-out dishcloth, or a withered prune, while at the same time pulsing with magick like an overcharged battery — even I was not tempted to argue.

I WILL SPARE YOU an account of our somewhat ragged journey back into Farringale. Let's just say that breaking my chair to bits and then clumsily shoving it back together did little to improve its navigational capabilities. Since I was also bashed up myself, and remained so despite Rob's hasty magickal medicine, I cannot say that I enjoyed the experience much.

As we trailed away, forming a straggling line across the sky, those great, roiling storm-clouds shifted; bright lightning flashed; and out came the griffins. They remained aloof from us this time, distant shapes soaring far overhead, wheeling upon the winds. An occasional, hollow cry drifted down to us below, a piercingly lonely sound.

Liberating some more treasures from their enchanted glass houses proved more difficult than we were hoping. Even Rob's splendid glass-breaking trick proved ineffectual when performed outside of a magickal surge, magick-soaked as he was. They had their uses, it seemed, even if they did render one too squiggly to easily take advantage.

So, we waited. I sat on the floor in one corner of the vaulted hall, feeding porridge alternately to myself and Ms. Goodfellow (it wasn't half bad, after all, though it could have done with a liberal lacing of chocolate spread). I tipped the contents of my satchel over the marble tiles and surveyed the loot.

One Mauf, previously acquired.

One hand-written book, apparently written in gibberish.

One set of memoirs, penned by the mysterious Lady Tregawny.

One as-yet-unidentified scroll in jewelled case, courtesy of Pup.

'You know what confuses me about this place?' I said after a while, but no one answered. Jay had wandered off to the other side of the wide hall, and applied himself to a study of some of the titles shelved there. Indira was floating in a chair somewhere over my head, scrutinising the long rows of glass-bound treasures (or Treasures?) stored farther up. 'They aren't all books!' she had announced some minutes before, and then maintained a steady report of her findings: 'A bunch of keys. A... hat, or something. Can't tell. Oh, a crown!' My ears pricked up at the word "crown", especially when it was shortly followed by: 'A few Wands, a sceptre, orb...'

Hmm.

'It's the fact that everything is so well-kept,' I continued, even if no one was listening. 'Look at it. Dust-free, grimeless. All right, so the Sweeping Symphony would keep that under control. But it's more than that. It's like the Starstone Spire in here. These books are insufficiently aged. Same goes for the furniture, the buildings themselves — the only signs of decay we've seen are an occasional stagnant puddle and some day-to-day level building deterioration. I mean, look at this.' I opened the hand-written journal with its pretty jade covers. 'This has to have been written hundreds of years ago, but the ink hasn't faded at all. I could conclude that someone put a pretty powerful preservation charm on it, but would that last so long, or so well? And has someone done the same with *every single object* in this entire city? I think not.

'Then there's the ortherex. Those surges of magick might explain why they're still here, but I doubt it. If they could thrive on nothing but magick alone, why do they bother with trolls at all? If there are no living hosts left here, then they cannot breed, and should have died off long ago.' I'd had some of these questions lurking at the back of my mind for weeks, without arriving at any particular conclusions. Now they were really piling up.

Jay drifted nearer. 'You're not veering back to that time travel theory, are you?'

'No. Not quite that.'

'Not quite?' Jay propped himself upon my chosen wall and surveyed my little haul thoughtfully. 'You're right, of course. I've been wondering the same things.'

I banged my head back against the wall in frustration. '- *Why* is there no information on this? It's maddening. And I could go on. The griffins. Why are they still here? Is it just that, with Farringale being closed off, no one could get in to hunt them down? It might be that simple, but then again maybe not. And what if my tossed-off suggestion was right? What if they are the same ones that were here when Farringale fell? What would that mean?'

'Either they live an incredibly long time,' Jay said. 'Or, like everything else in here, they apparently don't age.'

'That's it.' I pointed a finger at Jay, sitting up straighter. 'That's it. Is everything incredibly well preserved *in spite of* the passage of time, or is it not *experiencing* the passage of time? If nothing ages, is it because the process has been interfered with, or is it simply not happening at all?'

'You mean time doesn't pass in Farringale? No. It must, or why would there be any need for the Sweeping Symphony? How would those stagnant puddles develop?'

I gnawed a fingernail. 'Maybe it does, but just... not much of it. Maybe it's still pretty much 1658 in here.'

'Ves, you can't put a stasis enchantment on an entire city.'

'*I* can't, no, and neither could you. I'm pretty sure none of us could pull that off now. But we're talking about centuries ago, before the decline of magick. And, we're talking about a city that's drenched in so much magick it's drowning in it. Was it impossible *here,* so many years ago? Oh! You know what else, that would sort of explain how Baroness Tremayne's still here, too. Or was, the last time.'

I remain, whispered the Baroness, so near to my ear that I jumped with a shriek.

'What?' Jay said, scrambling towards me. But he was too slow. By the time he reached the spot I'd been sitting in, I was gone.

20

Baroness Tremayne lived *between the echoes*, as she had once put it. Then again, did she in fact live? Her insubstantial shadow world bore little resemblance to the vivid reality I knew. She'd pulled me sideways, as she had done before, and landed me in the middle of it, with all its darkness and distracting, flickery lights. I was still in the vaulted hall, but in some blurred, altered version. Between the echoes. I still did not understand quite what that meant.

The baroness, unchanged, regarded me gravely. She wore the same wide-skirted silk gown, ruffled with lace; the same artfully piled and curled arrangement graced her white hair. 'How curious a mind,' she said. 'Why do you return here? Did I not already satisfy your needs?'

'Oh! Yes,' I said, watching Jay out of the corner of my eye. He was prowling the hall, searching for me, his form shadowed and his movements jerky in my vision. 'May we invite my companion to join the conversation?'

The baroness did not even blink, but in the next moment Jay stood beside me.

'Jay, this is Baroness Tremayne,' I said. 'The lady who gave us the cure. Baroness, my colleague from the Society, Jay Patel.'

It felt a touch peculiar, making so mundane an introduction under such unusual circumstances. But Jay took it with aplomb. He made the baroness a bow, and flashed one of his more charming smiles. 'You saved many lives, ma'am.'

'I could not have done so without you to carry my aid to the afflicted, hence I suffer your presence now.' She spoke coldly. 'But you trespass, and you steal. What is it you now want from my poor Farringale?'

'We are here by royal command,' I said quickly. 'Their Majesties at the newer court, Mandridore, seek to learn more of the fate of Farringale, and sent us to discover what we could.' I opted to keep the other part of their vision, the restoration of the city, to myself for the time being. First things first, and how might the prickly baroness react to the idea?

'And what is your success?'

Any hopes she might be eager to tell all evaporated on the spot. 'Well, we have some theories—'

'As I heard.'

'Are they... accurate?'

The baroness just looked at me. At last she said: 'What will become of this knowledge, if 'tis given to you?'

'Ah... that would be up to Their Majesties,' I said tactfully.

Baroness Tremayne said nothing. I could not even tell if she was thinking it over. Her face was impassive.

'If I may ask,' Jay stepped in. 'Why do you linger, Baroness? By whose will, or order?'

'And, how?' I added.

The baroness drew herself up. 'I remain by order of Her Majesty, Queen Hrruna, and His Majesty King Torvaston.'

I exchanged a look with Jay, my heart leaping with excitement. I saw the same hope reflected in his face. But gently, gently; the baroness was wary. 'Are you here to care for the place?' I suggested.

Her lips quirked. 'Care for a dead land? What would be the use, pray?'

'It isn't dead, though, is it?' said Jay. 'Its people are gone, but the city goes on. The magickal surges. The griffins. The Sweeping Symphony — is that your doing? Everything has changed, and yet, nothing.'

'And nothing has aged,' I said. '*Nothing*. Including you.'

'Requires life, to grow older,' said she. 'The life poured out of Farringale long ago, and from me.'

'You're an echo,' I said. 'Are you? Though we might term it a shade.'

'Matters the word so greatly?'

Fair point.

'Baroness,' said Jay. 'Please. Tell us what happened when Their Majesties left Farringale.'

'Her Majesty required a promise of me, and I will keep it. I shall not tell.'

'Was it Torvaston, the king?' I probed. 'He was... ill, wasn't he? He and many of the Court. Magick-drowned, like Farringale itself.'

Her eyes flicked to me, but still she did not speak. I thought she grew more still and silent with every word I spoke.

Jay said, 'If Farringale lives on, it is Their Majesties' doing, and by Their will. It must be. Who else could wield such influence over this place? And they set you and others like you to watch over it all the long ages through. Why? It is because they did not want it to pass out of existence forever. They were trying to preserve it, Baroness, weren't they? For the future. And we come here by order of Their Majesties' descendants. They want to restore it to the world. If that day comes, your long vigil will be over and you may rest. Knowing this, will you not help us?'

Baroness Tremayne, caught between a promise to a long-dead queen and a command from the current one, grew hostile. 'You come from Their Majesties, in sooth? How do I know it to be so? You are mere adventurers. Already you divest Farringale of its treasures.'

I thought guiltily of the jade-coloured book and the jewelled scroll case. 'We carry some part of those treasures back to the new Court,' I said. 'And we are no adventurers. How, if so, do we come to be here at all? There is but one door to Farringale that ever opens now, and there are three keys to open it. Two remain with the Court, as I think you know well, Baroness. How came we to get those keys — not once, but twice — without the Court's approval? You must know how impossible it must be to take them without it.'

'And that door is significant, too,' said Jay. 'Why leave a way back at all, unless someone, someday, was supposed to use it?'

The mystery of the third key flitted, once more, across my mind. Why did House have the third key? How was it that the Baroness Tremayne knew our House well, as she'd previously claimed? Had someone, so long ago, foreseen the Society, and intended that it should be involved in the ultimate saving of Farringale?

That was absurd, wasn't it? How could it possibly be so?

I gave my head a shake to clear it. One problem at a time, Ves. (Or, more accurately, seven or eight).

To my intense disappointment, the baroness did not speak again. She looked from Jay to me, visibly torn — and then, with a thin, whispering sigh, faded away. Jay and I found ourselves blinking in the bright light of the hall, the shadowed echoes dissolved around us.

'Damn,' said Jay softly.

I was inclined to agree — until I noticed Rob, standing in the middle of the hall with a huge tome in his hands. Another lay at his feet. Both were bound in dark leather, with polished silver hinges.

'Ouch,' he said.

'Ouch?' I echoed.

'Came looking for you. Fell over these. We can add "books appearing out of nowhere" to the list of Farringale's oddities.'

As one, Jay and I rushed over there to look.

The title page of the book Rob held read as follows:

A Treatise Upon Magicke: Its Sources and Histories, penned by Torvaston Brandilowe.

'From before he became king?' said Jay. 'He was a scholar?'

'Not just any scholar,' said Rob, holding the book steady as I carefully turned pages. 'This is about ebbs and flows — what we're calling surges, is my guess.'

'And the whole question of Dells and their sources or fonts,' I added, speedily scanning pages. 'We have nothing like this.'

Jay squatted down to examine the second book. Smaller than the first, it had a shabbier look about it, as though it had been more regularly used: the leather of its bindings was worn in places, and some of the page edges ragged. 'Looks like a journal,' Jay reported. 'The author doesn't identify him or herself, but the handwriting's the same.'

Torvaston's own diary. My heart beat quick with excitement. What a prize! 'Written in Court Algatish,' I said. 'Archaic usage, naturally. Val and I would need a few weeks alone with these to wring the sense out of them.'

Indira dropped lightly down beside me, descended from somewhere above, and her hands weren't empty either. She carried a heavy crown, wrought from some metal I did not recognise: it looked coppery, but brighter, and also vivid gold, and somehow silvery as well. Plus, like any good royal crown, it positively blazed with jewels.

'How did you get that?' I gasped.

'I... didn't? It fell into my hands.'

We all turned to look up at the distant walls where Indira had lately flitted. One of the glass compartments was empty, its glass front not so much broken as absent.

'Our thanks, Baroness,' said Jay, echoed quickly by me.

'Right,' I said. 'I think we've got enough, for the time being. Let's go home.'

As may be imagined, the crown in particular caused a sensation back at Mandridore, though I think its effects upon Alban were mixed. Like his adoptive parents, Their Majesties the Royals, he gazed at it with the starry-eyed awe one cannot help feeling in the presence of something so fabulously beautiful and expensive — and, in this case, significant. But in him I detected a trace of dismay, too. Would this ornament, heavy with precious metals and duty alike, someday adorn his head?

Upon our arrival at Their Majesties' retreat house, we'd been greeted with rapture. By the time we'd arrived, the hour was far advanced and night long since fallen; but if we had turfed our royal employers out of bed, they made no sign of it.

It was just Jay and me again, too. Rob had elected to take Indira home, somewhat to her irritation, but he was right. We weren't justified in hauling Indira (or Rob either) across the country at three in the morning.

'Successful venture then, Ves?' Alban had said when he had collected us from Farringale's doorstep. I'd fallen into his car, bruised and laden with loot, and groaned.

'Fabulously,' I grinned, thrilled despite the bruises. Jay was right behind me, carrying the larger of the two tomes Rob had fallen over, with the crown set atop.

The baron's — *prince's* — brows rose into his hairline at that.

An hour or so later, we'd been plied with refreshments (to my relief), and sat ensconced with Their Majesties in their favourite parlour, our acquisitions set carefully upon a low walnut table nearby. Their Majesties, for a time lost for words, were beginning to rally.

'We haven't had chance to read the books closely yet,' I said. 'You might do so more speedily than we. And that one — the little green one — is still indecipherable. I think it's magick-drunk. As is the scroll case, which inexplicably contains zero scrolls because it's occupied by a silver fork, a gilded pocket-watch and a snuff box with a picture of a rather sexy troll lady enamelled into its lid.' I'd had some time to work on the sealed ends during the drive back to Mandridore, and had at last prised them off.

'We will have them studied and deciphered,' King Naldran assured me, politely glossing over the snuff box.

'These are wondrous finds,' said Her Majesty Ysurra, her usually rather dull eyes shining with excitement. 'This is Torvaston's crown, is it not? I believe it must be. My husband's is said to be the very same once worn at Farringale, but I have always thought that to be false. It has not the look of such an heirloom. A replica.'

'I begin to suspect that everything contained in that hall belonged to Torvaston or Hrruna, or was of some importance at Court,' I said.

'It does have the air of a museum,' Jay agreed. 'They knew they would have to leave a little before the final crisis, of course — what we know of Farringale's fall always said its decline took place over several months. So they prepared a sort of memorial hall. It's another item in support of our theory that they were trying to save something for the future. I think they hoped someone would someday find the way back.'

'Though,' I put in thoughtfully, 'why put Torvaston's crown there? Even if Torvaston himself wasn't to join his wife at Mandridore, the crown could have been passed on to the next heir.'

'A salient question,' said King Naldran. 'And there are so many.'

'Why did they not destroy the griffins?' said Queen Ysurra. 'If, as you propose, they are the source of these magickal surges?'

I tried to imagine the stone heart that could destroy so much majesty, and failed. 'I believe it was an arrangement that worked well for the city, for many years,' I said. 'They celebrated the surges, and made use of them. Only at the end did it... get out of hand, and the ortherex descended. We still do not know quite what happened.'

King Naldran nodded. 'And who would not wish for such a magickal surplus, from time to time, if it could be harnessed in some way?' He paused, but not in thought. He surveyed me, and subsequently Jay, with a speculative air.

Alban — seated, I had noted, much farther away from me than might previously have been his wont — smiled faintly at his father. 'You had better tell them,' he said.

The king nodded, but it was the queen who spoke. 'We hoped you would be successful, though you have far exceeded our expectations,' she said. 'We have a proposition for you, if you will hear it.'

'Say on,' said Jay, and I nodded.

The queen hesitated. 'We understand you to be without fixed employment at present. But, it has also become apparent that your ties with the Society remain strong. Perhaps we have been misinformed?'

Tricky question. 'It's complicated,' I said.

'Ah. Our idea was predicated upon the former, and it is thus: if you indeed seek to begin anew as your own entity, the Court would like to fund your enterprise, and bring it under our aegis.'

I was too surprised to speak. Whatever I might have anticipated by way of reward (if that's what it was), this wasn't it.

'Forgive me,' said Jay, more astute than I was. 'May I ask why?'

Queen Ysurra inclined her stately head. 'We have long admired the Society's work, and its... unusual methods. And it is apparent that the Court could benefit greatly from a similar force, particularly if we wish to pursue the question of Farringale. Since our various goals may be fulfilled by the same means, I propose this solution for us both.'

What to say? It was a generous offer, and would have been perfect — if it weren't for the fact that our secession from the Society had only ever been a sham.

Alban knew that, of course, or he'd guessed. I looked for a moment at him, but he gazed blandly back, giving me nothing. What was he up to?

'I think we couldn't accept,' said Jay. 'As you say, our ties with the Society remain strong...' He, no more than I, could find a simple way of explaining that we'd been lying through our teeth.

Alban's tiny, cynical smile appeared. 'They're still Society folk, mother. I did tell you.'

The queen sighed. 'Unfortunate.'

'Perhaps not,' I said. 'We have no real desire to set up independently, but that doesn't mean we can't help each other here. Why not form a partnership with the Society? You may assemble a joint force to work on the Farringale problem, of which we could conceivably be a part. And,' I added, with a wry smile of my own, 'I think we'd need their help anyway. After all, they've got the third key.'

Queen Ysurra did not look entirely happy about that last part, which intrigued me. 'So they do. We will think upon your suggestion, Miss Vesper.'

'With,' put in Alban, 'the firm intention of finding it an exceptionally good idea.'

'Though I'll add this: any restoration plan involving the destruction of those griffins is unlikely to find favour, either with us or with the rest of the Society.'

The queen looked down her royal nose at me, but she nodded.

So, that was that. I made a private resolve to pump Milady for information about that third key, next time I got the chance. How was it that the Society came to have it — and why had Baroness Tremayne claimed to know our House so well? Problems to pursue later.

Course, it also turned out *later* that the pocket-watch was Torvaston's and served a more complicated purpose than merely telling the time; the snuff box contained a signet ring, though not a royal one; and the inside of the scroll case was etched with a map of the Seas of Segorne on one half and the Vales of Wonder on the other. The plot, as they say, promptly thickened.

But that's a story for later, because what happened next was the one thing guaranteed to derail the Life of Ves in pretty short order.

My phone rang.

This may seem like a disappointingly mundane occurrence considering the build-up I've just given it, but it all comes down to who was on the other end.

'Ves,' I said crisply. I don't usually answer my phone that way, but this was a number I didn't recognise.

'Cordelia?'

It was a woman's voice, one I hadn't heard in years.

'I do not know why you insist on calling yourself by that peculiar abbreviation,' continued the voice. 'I gave you the most beautiful name I could think of.'

'...Mother?' I croaked.

'Hello, dear.'

Dear? Since when was I dear? 'How did you get this number?' I said, turning my back on Jay, whose expression of incredulity was just too much to be borne.

'I have spoken to Milady.'

'Milady gave you my number?'

'I needed to speak to you.'

'Wait. How do you know Milady?'

'Honestly, Cordelia. Everyone knows Milady. Now, listen. I need you to come here at once, and bring those pipes of yours.'

'My...' I paused to breathe. 'My pipes? How do you know about my pipes?'

'I consulted the register of known Great Treasures and their present owners. Imagine my surprise to find your name on the list! And it couldn't be more perfect. Bring the pipes, and the Waymaster. I'll see you soon.'

'Mother—' I began, using what has sometimes been termed my dangerous voice. For one thing, that list is privileged access only, it's not like you can just Google it or something. For another, how dare she call me out of the blue and propose to haul me off to goodness-knew-where?

And what was Milady doing enabling her?

But she'd ended the call. I uttered a few choice expletives, and ended up glowering darkly at Jay.

'Your mother doesn't have your number?' He could've said, *you've got five lungs and a double spleen?* in approximately the same tone.

'It's complicated.'

'I see that.'

I took a deep breath. 'We appear to have a change of plans.'

Also By Charlotte E. English

Modern Magick

The Road to Farringale

Toil and Trouble

The Striding Spire

The Fifth Britain

Royalty and Ruin

Music and Misadventure

The Wonders of Vale

The Heart of Hyndorin

Alchemy and Argent
The Magick of Merlin
Dancing and Disaster

House of Werth

Wyrde and Wayward
Wyrde and Wicked
Wyrde and Wild

9 789492 824318